To the children of divorce

Contents

Part II
Co-Parenting Guidelines

Foreword

A funny thing happened on the way to the courthouse. Going to court daily with battling clients, we realized that there must be a better way to settle these disputes, especially when they involve children. There *is* a better way: bringing parents together in a nonthreatening, neutral environment without the win/lose of the courthouse. That is precisely what Drs. Thayer and Zimmerman discuss in this book. Their goal is to bring peace to the high-conflict family so that the children can thrive and grow with two parents working in concert, not at polar opposites.

The need for an instruction manual for high-conflict families is apparent to all of us who work in this field. Any number of lawyers, judges, clerks, and court service officers working in the milieu of the divorce court can relate horror story after horror story of insane disputes between families—disputes that appear to be so easily resolvable to those of us not involved. Why is it that these parents can't resolve it? How does this segment of the divorcing population get so enmeshed in the battle that, even for the sake of their children, they cannot disengage? Why are these parents more empowered by the battle than by peace?

Every day hundreds of couples decide to end their marriages and file for divorce. Some of those decisions are made thoughtfully and mutually, with or without the assistance of professionals, by couples who give careful attention to the myriad details that accrue to the breakup of a financial entity. Other endings are spontaneous and rapid, erupting onto the scene with the vigor of a gale force wind, leaving the parties breathless and unsure of their direction. Still others are violent, involving the intervention of state authority and the enforced separation of family members.

The same people who are seemingly normal and loving outside the courtroom may become uncontrollable within the court environment during the process of divorce. People who would never overtly hurt their children or anyone else willingly destroy their children's lives in order to "win." People who would never physically assault their children regularly assault their children's psyches.

Many parents, through trial and error, work things out between themselves, creating a new parenting arrangement. Other parents consistently fail to resolve the parenting issues between them. These become the high-conflict cases. The children of these divorces watch their parents turn the family inside out, as the parents move away from each other and into new homes, new jobs, new relationships. These parents cut old ties and reinvent themselves as "single parents." They are forced to create a new parenting plan with their former parenting partner. Formerly innocuous forms of communicating via the children ("Tell Daddy that dinner is ready") become negative and dangerous ("Tell your father his child support check is late again"). The children attempt to learn the new rules as they begin to move between the newly formed and continually evolving parental hemispheres. The separated or divorced adults now see themselves not only as single adults but also as single parents, often operating independently and in conflict with their former spouse.

Divorce does not produce "single" parents. Parents produce "single" parents. Divorce produces parents who live in separate houses. Divorce should not end a parent's involvement with the children. Parents should not lose decision-making powers, be it whether to pierce a child's ears or where the children will attend school. Yet, too often, that is precisely what happens through the divorce process. Someone is "in" and someone is "out." Someone "has" the children and someone doesn't. The losers are *always* the children.

The children we represent are a distinct class in the group of children of divorce. They are children caught in the maelstrom of the parental conflict—the drowning children, the alienated children, the children who have lost their parents to litigation. They are being raised by "divorcing adults" who will not make a parenting decision without legal advice. Our clients experience loud parental conflict in the home, at school, and on the soccer field. They may see the police come to their home to control their parents' arguments. They hold the secrets of one parent from the other parent. They attempt to split their childhood up to be fair to their parents. They, as children, deliver the child support checks. They spend their holidays on a rotating schedule between two homes, often cramming two or more holiday celebrations with extended family into a single day. They give up extracurricular activities and parties because they interfere with "Mom's time" or "Dad's time." These children are knowledgeable in the courts' treatment of men and women, in child support theory, in legal language and procedure. They can recite their parents' respective legal positions. They refer to their parents' attorneys by first name.

The high-conflict family asks a cumbersome, overburdened legal system to respond to and alleviate its distress. The courts replace the parents as decision makers for the children. No decision is too minute for the high-conflict parent to place before a judge. Motions are filed, evaluations are conducted, testimony is taken, and orders are entered. A legally sanctioned or court-ordered parenting plan is put into place and the high-conflict family is sent on its way. The court, the lawyers, and the legal safety net move on to new families.

Parents with badly damaged communication skills and a history of litigation are left to negotiate and interpret their court orders and deal with urgent circumstances not covered by the "orders." How do we resolve a conflict around our child's medical care? What if we don't agree on the need for orthodontia? Can a stepparent discipline our child? What if Billy is invited to a sleepover on Dad's weekend? High-conflict parents cannot address these parenting issues without stress, acrimony, and argument. Their children continue to suffer.

Parents with conflict, sometimes severe and at times less so, are the parents that Drs. Thayer and Zimmerman are addressing in this book.

The Co-Parenting Survival Guide offers these families a solution and a chance to move beyond the high-conflict divorce experience and produce a parenting system that allows the children to keep their family (albeit a reconstituted one). Drs. Zimmerman and Thayer focus on co-parenting the children even after the horrific divorce. Parents who have spent their recent history vilifying their spouse to anyone who will listen, including their children, *can* learn to return to a level of communication and exchange of information that will benefit their children. Parents *can* learn to put their issues aside and deal directly and fairly with one another for the good of the children. New rules and communication styles *can* be developed by the parents to accommodate the change in their marital status. *Co-parenting effectively after a high-conflict divorce is a reachable goal.*

Divorce is a reality in our society. Acrimony and hostility between parents, and attitudes that alienate and frighten their children, need not be a part of divorce. The joy of finding a book like *The Co-Parenting Survival Guide* is that it demonstrates to parents that they can choose to change their behavior toward the other parent. Parents can show their children that positive growth can result from divorce. Parents can be individual people and still be good parents after divorce. Parents need not live in the same house to retain their rights as parents. Children need not choose between one parent or the other in order to survive their parents' "war."

The Co-Parenting Survival Guide will help parents understand that they are not "single parents" but "co-parents," as they have been since their children were born. Every divorce attorney, family court judge, court service officer, and divorcing parent should be required to learn the contents of this book. Perhaps then the children of future divorces need not suffer the traumas our clients have suffered all these years.

Parents *can* undo their past errors. They *can* regroup and restructure their post-divorce parenting so that their children can grow up in a healthy, happy, and loving environment in both parents' homes.

Emily J. Moskowitz, Esq. & Jennifer E. Davis, Esq.

Acknowledgments

The authors would first like to thank all of the parents and children they have worked with during their careers. Your candor, trust, pain, and willingness to be vulnerable have taught us so much and have contributed to our understanding and to this work. Our work with high-conflict parents grew out of a sincere desire to create a more sensitive world for children and parents of divorce. We would also like to thank our practice colleagues and staff and our many attorney colleagues for sharing ideas and helping to guide us in our work with parents of high-conflict divorce. Attorneys Davis and Moskowitz have contributed not only the Foreword to this work but along with others have demonstrated their encouragement as we developed the P.E.A.C.E. Program for high-conflict parents. We would also like to thank New Harbinger Publications, whose editors had the foresight to take a risk on two unknown authors who presented the initial idea for this book in the aisle at a professional conference. We thank our families—Jack, John, and Rachel and Laura, Jonathan and Alison—for their support and patience during the long process of writing and editing. Finally, we are indebted to our own parents—Mignon, Bob, Shirley, and Joe—for teaching us about the meaning of parental love. This book has only become a reality with the help of all of you. Thank you.

Introduction

Your baby is born. What a remarkable day—one you will never forget. Your child grows, and you provide endless nurturance and love. You wake up at 2 A.M. to take care of your baby (even when *you* don't feel well). As your baby grows, you watch him or her mature in so many ways. Your infant learns to turn over, sits up, takes first steps, and begins to talk. Your young child goes to school, struggles with friends, and continues to grow and develop.

As time goes on you make countless decisions. Some are trivial and some are large. Some are easy and others are nerve-racking. Parenting is a most glorious and difficult job. But you aren't necessarily alone. This difficult job starts with a partner, one you get to choose.

At the start, you might have been quite thrilled with your choice. You may have entered marriage and/or parenthood with anticipation and excitement. However, parenting is only one part of a relationship, and as time went on your relationship deteriorated. In addition, your partner's commitment to parenting may have seemed stronger or weaker than yours. Communication may have faltered. There was a lack of support that weakened the "connection." Trust eroded. At some point, even though your child continued to grow and develop, your relationship with your partner began to end. Your child, who loves you both, had to hear, "Mommy and Daddy are getting a divorce."

Thus began one of the most stressful and painful experiences you have ever faced—disentangling from your spouse. In a divorce, extended family, money, possessions, friends, and homes divide or ally with one side or the other. Feelings of sadness, anger, anxiety, and depression can be frequent and intense. You may feel alone and vulnerable. The resentment grows. It can be surprising how angry and distrustful you feel. "How could I have ever loved this person?" is a frequent question. Unfortunately, the distrust and anger toward each other get expressed through the children, your last mutual connection.

Hostility and conflict develop. The ending of the relationship is often very adversarial. You may talk about it as a "battle." You disagree and argue over money, possessions, custody, visitation, discipline, and extracurricular activities for your children. The battle rages on. When is the next court date? What motions did my ex file? What are my countermotions? Telephone calls are at times "impossible." The legal documents pile up. What was once in a file folder now covers your dining room table and becomes all-consuming.

However, as time goes on, a plan emerges. The lawyers put together an agreement that both of you probably find less than ideal. A parenting and visitation plan is constructed. Finally, a judge pronounces that you are divorced. It's over. Or is it just beginning?

What happened to you and your ex during the battle? Did you become distracted at times? Did you feel emotionally wounded? Were there days when you wanted to give up? Was it hard to have enough energy to give? Did your child(ren) become more demanding or more needy? Did you get so used to litigation that you couldn't directly express your child's needs to the other parent? Did you spend day after day in court missing work and other commitments? Did you spend a fortune on litigation? Did you end up letting the court make decisions for your children that you should have made together as parents? Are you filled with so much animosity and distrust that you can hardly look at or talk with your ex without legal intervention?

It may be hard to remember this, but children's needs intensify during a divorce. They feel the stress and they experience the conflict. Their lives are turned upside down. They didn't ask for the divorce, but they're subjected to seeing the two people they love most engaged in a bloodless but at times bitter and devastating battle.

Many divorced parents say how much they love and how they "would do anything for" their children. But they have incredible difficulty when it comes time to communicate with each other about their children. Children need two parents who can work together—parents who can put aside the battle for the sake of the children.

Children continue to need the love, support, and guidance of both of their parents. They need the "partnership" of parenthood to continue in order to have the best chance of thriving and growing in a way that will enable them to be happy and develop healthy relationships in the future.

This book is written for parents who, in spite of their separation or divorce, want what is best for their children. It is written for parents who are caught in the battle of separation and divorce. It is for parents who feel that no matter what they do, they can't get their ex to be fair and reasonable with them or their child. It is for parents who are tired of fighting.

We also wrote this book to help your child. We believe that children need to be able to love and be loved by both their parents. Children need parents to work together (even though they have their own differences) to give them a stable, loving environment. Children need the battle not to involve them. They need to be taken out of the middle and loved by two parents who unfortunately no longer love each other.

This book will help teach you what you can do to work with your children's other parent. It will guide you and help you build a relationship as "co-parents." It offers specific and practical suggestions to decrease conflict, resolve differences, and help you parent your children. It is best read by both parents, so each of you can work on changing your own (not each other's) behavior. In this regard, you might also find it useful to read this book with a journal or notepad by your side, so you can record thoughts and ideas that may be helpful to you.

Part I of this book describes an overall philosophy and general guidelines for building an effective co-parenting relationship in spite of the conflict. We focus on unique strategies for co-parenting that can be implemented even when conflict and litigation have been a consuming concern. Part II addresses specific challenges of high-conflict co-parents and gives practical suggestions for getting down to the business of co-parenting. The needs of co-parenting may be similar for all parents, but the challenge to obtain resolution is much more intense for parents with high conflict. In these families, decisions concerning daily care can be as monumental as changes in the visitation plan. Parents can learn about communication traps and ways to avoid the cycle of endless battles. Throughout this book we use many examples that are based on real cases. However, they have been disguised to protect the identities of individual parents and children. The situations and principles they discuss are common, but the specific details have been altered.

This book is written for those battle-fatigued families who need to make major changes for the sake of their children. Making the commitment to end the battle and begin co-parenting is the largest step you can take to care for your children. Your children need *two* loving and caring parents. This is far more important than winning the battle, proving a point to your ex, or protecting yourself from feeling used. Our hope is that you read this book with your children (not your ex) in mind. Think about what childhood memories and feelings you want to give them. You *can* give yourselves back to your children as parents. They *can* have the love of both their parents—even after the divorce.

Part I

Conflict and Parenting: A Difficult Combination

CHAPTER 1

Are You Addicted to Conflict?

The Dying Marriage

It Can Happen Slowly

It starts subtly. First, there may be an argument or a sense of disregard. You or your partner may think, "I'm just not understood." The argument and "disconnects" are painful and disturbing but you get past them.

"He/she just doesn't understand me. Why don't they get it? I keep explaining myself, but it's not doing any good. I hate arguing. Talking doesn't help. Maybe it would be better to just leave it alone and not keep getting us both upset."

Time passes and there are more misunderstandings. There are more arguments, hurt builds and distrust grows. Often, issues that need to be discussed are avoided in an attempt not to argue yet again. Talking on a day-to-day basis becomes more superficial. It becomes focused on the "doing" and not on feelings, and the distance between you grows and grows.

These are often signs of a marriage in trouble. At this point you might try to rationalize your way out of the stress and pain by saying, "Nobody's marriage is perfect. Why should I expect mine to be? I have beautiful children. So what if I'm not happy?" Unfortunately, this rationalization only helps on a short-term basis. It may help you get through the day, but does not address the problems in the relationship.

Relationships can be thought of as living entities. Like plants, they need attention. They need to be nurtured. If the relationship isn't nurtured it wilts. It can often be brought back to life, but if ignored for too long it begins to die. Avoiding the pain caused by failing communication means ignoring the relationship, which then wilts and begins to die anyway.

Most of us aren't interested in experiencing pain. By definition it is unpleasant and therefore something we naturally try to avoid. However, by avoiding the pain in a relationship, we avoid each other. As the distance increases, the joint communication, the sharing, and the feeling of "us" slowly erode. You may become more self-protective.

"I'm not going to try (or say) that again. All that does is cause more pain." As you become more self-protective it becomes more difficult to trust your partner. You go through the motions of daily life, but emotionally share less and take fewer risks. You wall yourself off from your partner. Rather than talk about the simple decisions, you might say, "I'll just take care of it myself. It's not worth fighting about it." Quite likely, your partner is going through a similar process and is becoming more distant from you as well. This serves to increase the speed of the decline. It's like two trains traveling in opposite directions—as time passes, they quickly become farther and farther apart.

As communication fails and trust declines, couples focus more and more on taking care of themselves as individuals but not as partners. They become more "I" focused. Day-to-day decisions become more difficult. Simple decisions become minor squabbles or even full-blown arguments. There is an escalation of minor conflicts, which can become major disputes. There is more hurt, more distrust, and more distance, and the relationship continues to wither.

The relationship begins to die as hopelessness sets in. "He/she will never change and will never understand me. I will never be happy or cared for in this marriage. How can I go on living like this?" Hopelessness sometimes leads to attempts to bring the relationship back to life. Counseling, weekends away, long talks, tears, doing "nice things" may all be attempts to breathe life back into the relationship. However, often these attempts are not successful in shifting the focus from individual needs to nurturing the relationship in a sustained manner. Guilt, anger, and depression may also set in as the relationship continues to falter. Resentment about the misunderstandings and disconnects continues to grow. You or your partner may become more distant and more self-protective. The sense of "aloneness" may be overwhelming. You may say to yourself, "We've been married all this time, but I don't know this person lying next to me at night. Who are they? I can't believe it came to this. All of our hopes and dreams. Being alone would be better than this. At least we wouldn't be hurting each other anymore. I just can't stand this. I can't stand what we've become. This has got to end. It's not good for either of us. It's not good for the children." The marriage dies as the process of divorce begins in full.

The Traumatic End

Many marriages end as a result of a major, traumatizing betrayal. While these marriages may have had early warning signs, the turning point is often thought to be a single major incident or discovery of a betrayal in trust. Some common incidents include:

- Discovery of another relationship (affair, long-standing meaningful relationship, second family)

- Significant betrayal about money (hidden accounts and assets, gambling addiction, stock market losses)

- Awareness of a major deceit (sexual addiction, job problems, criminal record, sexual orientation)

- Sudden separation (one person suddenly announces they are going to leave)

These and other situations all share a common theme: the disclosure or discovery of a secret, which is deemed to be a betrayal of the central trust of the relationship. Not all relationships end at this point. Some may see this as a turning point to reexamine themselves and their interaction patterns. They may begin a healing process and even get stronger. However, many marriages end at this time (or some time later) as they are not able to heal or rebuild. "I can't believe it!" and "I can't take it!" are common responses. There is often a sense of a major and fatal wound to the integrity of the marriage. One person may think, "What was I doing here? Was this all an act? Was it all a sham?"

The other spouse might say, "I was trying to hold our marriage together the best I could. I didn't want to disclose the secret because I thought it would lead to our falling apart. I guess I was right because here we are. We *are* falling apart."

When a marriage ends traumatically, there can be a sense of shock and disbelief. It is as if a loved one dies suddenly. "This can't be happening to me" is a common response. Denial can play a role. There can be a period of trying to save or rescue the marriage. "If I just try hard enough, we can keep this going." There may be a period of increased sexual connection, increased communication, or more time together. However, if the "trying" does not lead to healing and new and sustained interaction patterns, the marriage may nevertheless be doomed.

At some point, one or the other parent decides to end the marriage. Pain, anger, hurt, and resentment can return at full force. "How could you do this to me? How could you do this to the children?" is often the response of the one who feels injured or betrayed.

"How could I do this? This is why I did it. Look at your reaction. This is exactly what I expected. I knew you wouldn't [or couldn't] understand. I knew you would behave like this. You're impossible to deal with," says the other spouse.

Here again, the battle lines are drawn. In this case, one parent may adopt the role of "victim," while the other parent assumes the role of the misunderstood spouse who tried unsuccessfully to "hold it all together." Each side then perceives that they alone are the victim. They view each other as a victimizer and at fault as they *both* say, "How could you do this to me?"

The Marriage That Never Was

The love, passion, and emotion are intense. There is a pregnancy and a child is born. There is not a legal marriage, but perhaps you live together. Perhaps the relationship ends before the pregnancy is discovered, or perhaps it ends during the pregnancy. There may or may not have ever been a committed relationship. Fortunately, both parents recognize and feel the responsibility to the child. But the parents may have differing levels of responsibility and commitment to the pregnancy and child. In addition, they may not have a long history of togetherness behind them.

You might think that this would put them at a disadvantage. How can two people who don't know each other well successfully engage in the complicated task of co-parenting? At times, the conflict can also be less because the "connection" is less. These parents may actually be more objective and more reasonable because there is less of an emotional or subjective viewpoint. On the other hand, their conflict can be more intense due to a lack of long-term concern and caring for the other parent. It is more like negotiating and working with an assigned partner.

The Legal System

Did You Hire a Warrior?

"I'll just go to a lawyer for some information. You know, everyone tells me I just need to understand my rights. I shouldn't do anything stupid that would put the children or me at a disadvantage. I just want to get this thing over with as quickly as possible." Even if you enter the legal arena with a sincere intention to keep things from getting too complicated, the process of disentangling a relationship is far from simple. There are financial considerations, with related discussions about dividing assets, mortgages, loans, IRAs, mutual funds, profit-sharing plans, child support, and alimony. Custody, visitation, education, and medical concerns are but a few of the complicated issues that are often discussed with the attorney.

You eventually hire a lawyer whom you feel will best represent *your* interests. Your spouse does the same. You pay this professional to help you, protect your interests, and at times, to get back at your spouse. You might be thinking, "If she/he thinks I'm going to make this easy on them, they've got another thing coming. I don't want this divorce. I didn't ask for it and I'm not going to end it without a fight." Or you might be thinking, "I'll never get out of this divorce alive. My partner has always been the strong one in this relationship. Look how many times I've been manipulated or hurt in this relationship. Now that we're getting divorced it's only going to be more of the same. My lawyer had better fight for me or I'm going to wind up with nothing."

The conflict escalates as your lawyer appropriately advises you of your rights and discusses the process of divorce. Relevant case law and precedents may be discussed with you. The "best case" and "worst case" scenarios are described to you. You begin to examine how to position yourself legally to avoid the "worst case" scenario and possibly enhance the chances of winding up with the "best case." Unfortunately, your soon-to-be-ex is doing the very same thing. Financial affidavits and other documents have to be produced. Strategy sessions may be held. There may even be an initial meeting, a "four-way," with the two of you and your attorneys.

Often, the four-way does not go well. It can feel as if both sides are checking each other out. There is positioning and you hear ultimatums. Each side tells the other that they are being unreasonable. It is almost as if the warriors are lining up on each side of the battlefield as they prepare for the conflict ahead. You may be glad you chose the lawyer you did and think, "I knew this wasn't going to be easy. I can't believe how difficult my spouse is being. He/she is so unreasonable. I'm really glad I hired this attorney. It's a lot of money but it will be well spent. He/she will take care of me."

Guess what? Your partner is probably having the same experience. You are less alone than you realize. Both of you may be in the same place, squaring off for a battle. You may be paying your attorneys to engage in conflict—paying your attorneys to fight for you so that you don't "lose."

But think about it this way: You are one family. You may be individual adults, but you are one family with one set of assets. There are children whom you will always share. If one of you wins and one of you loses, is there really a true victory? If one parent is conquered in the battle, can that be good for the children? Can children possibly benefit from knowing the devastation that each parent experiences at the hands of the other? Can children possibly avoid being caught in the crossfire on the battlefield? Can they benefit from having one or both parents financially and/or emotionally wounded by the other parent? How can they reconcile or understand that one parent, whom they love, will try to hurt the other parent whom they also love?

Mediation

Perhaps, recognizing this dilemma, you and your partner search out an alternative. One well-known alternative is mediation. While you and your spouse may still have your own attorneys, you both work jointly with a third attorney who attempts to help the two of you reach a fair and reasonable divorce settlement and agreement. The mediation attorney will also work on constructing a reasonable parenting plan to address custody, visitation, and other needs of the children.

Collaborative Divorce

Collaborative divorce is a second alternative to the traditional divorce. The collaborative divorce process involves attorneys, financial experts, and therapists jointly working with the parents (and children). They strive to avoid conflict, agree not to litigate, and try to reach equitable solutions while being very attentive to the needs of the children. They also focus on helping build communication, problem-solving, and conflict-resolution skills so you can better work together during and after the divorce.

Both of these alternatives work for many partners who are getting divorced. However, at times the conflict is so intense and the trust is so completely eroded that compromise, negotiation, and collaborative communication are not feasible. In these cases, the conflict surpasses the ability of the parents and the related professionals to contain it. These parents enter into an unfortunate high-conflict divorce process.

The Divorce

We often marry for the first time as young adults—barely out of childhood. We think we understand the world and ourselves when we make one of the most important decisions of our lives in the midst of excitement, social pressures, anxiety, love, and passion. We have hopes, expectations, and dreams.

At some point during the divorce process we realize that those dreams are far from realized. "I *had* a dream" becomes the speech you might be telling yourself. Your partner is saying the same thing. Each of you had dreams as you dated and married and had children. Those dreams are gone. Rarely on the day the divorce is finalized does anyone say, "I'm happy. I've completed that goal. Boy, do I feel good." Perhaps most surprising is that many people do not even feel they've won. In an adversarial process we would expect there to be winners and losers. Half of those people who are divorced should feel like winners. Why don't they?

They don't feel like winners because in a divorce everyone loses. Everyone loses dreams. In fact, you may feel the amount of loss that you would feel if you were grieving the loss of a loved one. That is because you (and your ex) *are* grieving the loss of a loved one! Actually, you have lost many loved ones. First, you have lost a love partner. This loss may have happened over time and the grief may have been experienced as a slow and gradual process. Second, there is the loss of the relationship. In addition to loving your partner, you may have loved being "in love" or being married. Third, you most probably lost time with your children. Fourth, you have witnessed the losses your children have sustained during the divorce. Fifth, there is the loss of money and tangible assets. This loss often preoccupies high-conflict parents.

Children of high-conflict divorce have not escaped the grief and hurt. They have watched their parents hurt each other. They have lost family time. They have lost the ease of having access to both parents. They have lost their dreams and expectations of having an intact family, and they have lost their innocence. Because children often feel responsible for their parents' divorce and continued conflict, they may have also lost a sense of being free to be children—to play, laugh, and have fun with peers and family. Children will often say, "I should have been able to stop it" or "I should be able to get my parents back together." No matter how successful you may feel as you divorce, your children are the ultimate losers. Except in extreme and unsafe circumstances, children lose more than they gain during a divorce (especially a divorce filled with conflict).

The divorce has shattered the dreams of everyone in the family. It *is* a sad and painful time. By the time the divorce is legally finalized, you may be wishing to just get on with your life and leave some of the pain behind.

After the Divorce

Well, it's finally over and you can now get on with your life. You have a parenting plan and the visitation and custody have finally been worked out. The financial issues have been decided. This new chapter of your life and your children's lives can now begin; the healing can start now that the battle has ended.

With this "new beginning" you may even find a bit of energy and excitement. You may change your living space around, get rid of those horrid things your ex just loved, and even tell the children, "this is the beginning of a new time for us as a family." You have new dreams and hopes. You think, "As long as my ex sticks to the agreement, everything will be fine. I *can* do this." By the way, your ex is probably thinking the same thing.

Unfortunately, these hopes may not be easily realized. Your relationship with your ex did not improve the day the judge signed the divorce decree. Your communication skills did not improve. The distrust and hurt did not evaporate. The reality is that as you and your ex begin to try on these new roles as divorced parents, you find that there are more disappointments.

Your ex is not reasonable about trivial variations from the initial parenting plan. Aunt Eloise from Toledo is coming into town Wednesday night. She wants to see you and the children. You call your ex and ask if you can switch nights so the children can see Aunt Eloise. Your ex says it won't work out because he/she has made plans to take the children "elsewhere" that evening. You don't believe this flimsy and vague excuse. You know your ex is just doing this to be mean.

You pick up your child on Saturday and are asked why you missed the soccer dinner at the local pizza parlor on Thursday night. Everyone's parents were there, including your ex. "Why couldn't you be there?" your child asks. You didn't know about the dinner because your ex didn't tell you.

You assume, no, you are certain, that these are attempts to get at you and make you look like a bad parent. You decide you must fight back. This isn't your usual attitude, so you're surprised at yourself—but what choice do you have?

So, it begins again. The miscommunication, the distancing, the disappointment all contribute to continued conflict. As the disagreements ensue, it becomes more and more difficult to implement the parenting plan. You find you are less willing to "give in" or be flexible. You communicate with your ex minimally or not at all. You may return to the lawyer's office for advice or to file postdivorce motions. The warring is supposed to be over, but no matter what you do, no matter what you try, the relationship still doesn't "work."

You can't believe there is still one injustice after another. Even your lawyer can't believe it and so you are told, "In all my years of practice I haven't seen anything like this. This is ridiculous. I can't believe the position your ex is taking." There are more motions, countermotions, and pretrial hearings. But there is no resolution and you find yourself still struggling through the swamp of conflict.

Conflict Addiction

As you struggle through the adjustments around divorce, the resentments and the emotional wounds do not necessarily leave just because you are no longer with your spouse. Instead, there may be constant reminders of the old hurts. There are also plenty of new opportunities for additional pain. Your partner was in charge of taking out the garbage or seeing to it that the children have the clothes they need and like. When you are taking the garbage out on your way to work, and the bag rips and there is tomato sauce on your suit and a mess on the ground, it is easy to resent your ex for putting you in this position. When you're trying to buy the children their sneakers and they whine and insist that they only want the expensive pair that is not as good for their feet, you may blame your ex. In fact, it is easy to resent your ex for just about everything.

As the resentment builds, it continues to reinforce the anger and the hurt. It makes it incredibly easy to be defensive and uncooperative. As your ex goes through similar feelings, cooperation seems impossible. Everything becomes a battle, and you want nothing to do with that person. You might think, "How could I have ever felt anything for him/her?" Yet you must have contact with your ex. Your children may talk about their time with their other parent. You have to coordinate pickups and transitions. The school may ask you both to attend a meeting. You need to change a visitation day or pickup time or alter visitation because of vacation plans.

The sample letters below show how easily the conflict escalates. Notice the subtle (and not-so-subtle) barbs and how the parents spend more energy on the battle than on solving the problems and attending to the children.

Dear Jane,

I am writing to address a couple of points. I thought I would write this time to avoid any chance that you would again misunderstand me.

First, I have repeatedly asked that you send church clothes with Susie on her weekends with me. She is a growing child. I send you child support and would hope that since she has clothes that she wears to church on her weekends with you, you would send those with her. For me to go out and buy nice clothes and shoes for her, to leave here for her to only grow out of, is a bit ridiculous and not financially prudent. I am sure this can be arranged and is not too difficult for you.

Second, in the future, I would appreciate it if you would let me know at least five days in advance when her school concerts are scheduled. I found out about the last one after I had scheduled a business dinner and could not make it. This is not right. It is bad for me and bad for Susie.

Third, I need to change the visitation for the weekend of June 26. I plan to be in Martha's Vineyard and will not be able to pick her up or deliver her back to you on time because of the ferry schedule. Our agreement is very specific about these things and I certainly do not want to be violating the judge's order. I could take her the weekend of July 4 or the next weekend if that is better for you.

I hope you can get back to me quickly on these matters. None of them are too complicated or too difficult.

Dick

cc: Betty Smith, Esq.

June 8, 1999

Dear Dick,

Thank you for your letter (although I am not sure when it was written). It is hard to misunderstand you when we have not spoken or communicated in any way for quite a while.

This is the first that I have heard of the church clothes issue. You have not discussed this with me directly but have talked with Susie about this numerous times. She is quite embarrassed about her outfits for church and naturally now doesn't want to go at all when she is with you. At her age she is constantly changing her mind about what she wants to wear. I suggest that you and she use the opportunity to bond by going shopping for one or two appropriate outfits for church. In addition, I no longer practice your religion and church with Susie is your own domain.

As for the concert issue, Susie brought home her concert notice in her backpack on one of your days. Since you failed to look in her bag then I guess you missed that notice. It would be important to check her bag daily for school papers and also notes that I write to you about homework status, etc. If you want to attend these events you may not always have five days notice and, like me, may have to change work commitments for Susie's sake.

The weekend of June 26 is not good for me either. I already have plans that take me out of town, so you will have to make other arrangements. Please let me know what you decide so I can let you know whether or not I approve of your new plans for Susie. The weekend of July

4 is my weekend and I will be taking Susie to Nantucket with me. John will be accompanying us with his two children. The next weekend begins my vacation week with Susie and so that will not be possible either. I think it is best that we don't change the agreed-upon schedule because flexibility just causes such confusion for Susie right now.

I agree that this is not very complicated so I too hope we can settle these issues soon. You can leave times when you can be reached on my voice mail, and I will be glad to call you back to discuss your concerns.

Jane

cc: Betty Smith, Esq.
    Tom Jones, Esq.

June 10, 1999

Dear Jane,

I am shocked and surprised! Why don't we communicate much? Well your letter to me is the reason. You begin your letter with the usual sarcastic shots and criticism of me. I wrote you to try to work out some important details and you respond not only without any consideration, but also with the nastiness typical of you during our marriage. When did you get the letter? It was written a day or two before—duh!

As a point of fact, you and I have discussed the clothing issue a number of times. As you may recall, it is your responsibility to send Susie with the clothes she needs for the weekend. If she is embarrassed it is your doing. It is quite obvious that your refusal to send an outfit for church is simply your way of putting our daughter in the middle so that you can get back at me. If you care that she is embarrassed (if that is even true) then I can't imagine why you wouldn't send the clothes that are hanging in her closet. What religion you practice is completely irrelevant to the point at hand.

For the record, I am perfectly willing to change my work schedule for Susie. I have done that for years—even when we were married. All I am asking is that you give me adequate notice. I routinely look through her papers and ask her if anything new is going on. I did not see that paper when I looked through her backpack and again strongly ask that you keep me informed of significant activities that she is involved in. This is part of our divorce agreement and I expect you to stick to it!

You are so inflexible and just want it all at any price. To change a couple of days is not impossible. You seem to have forgotten how I traded Easter and Thanksgiving so you could have Susie with your mother who was going to be in town. You seem to have forgotten the times that I let you take Susie on a Saturday to go to hobby shows that you say are so important. You're going to have Susie for the week. I can't understand why you don't show some flexibility here. If we have to go by the letter of our agreement from now on, then we can and I won't be flexible either. If we can't change weekends then my mother will come over and Susie will stay with her when I'm not home. By the way, I don't need your permission for that.

You say you hope we can settle these issues, but I don't see it. You're totally inflexible and condescending. Your attitude in your letter is the usual one that says everything will be fine if we just do things your way. If this is how you respond to me when you have time to think and react in writing, it will not be better by phone.

For the sake of our daughter (whom you say you love), I would ask you to reconsider the three points I raised in my first letter.

Dick

cc: Betty Smith, Esq.

June 11, 1999

Dear Dick,

It is very clear how much communication has broken down between us. Your style of name-calling is something that I should never have tolerated during our marriage but I certainly don't have to tolerate it now! You call me inflexible when it is you who always want the schedule changed. If you don't get your way, you yell and scream like usual. You are not thinking about Susie. You are only thinking about yourself and your convenience.

I am not your secretary anymore nor am I responsible for informing you about all of Susie's activities and schedule. No matter how many times I tell you what is going on you don't remember. I guess you still want me to keep track of things for you. Well, you can call the school and the soccer, piano, and dance places yourself to get the schedules and information.

The money you give me for Susie only goes so far and doesn't come near to covering all her expenses. We need to revisit our agreement if you expect me to supply all clothing and you none. You have no idea how much it costs to raise a child. You never took care of any of this during our marriage either.

Susie is caught in the middle here and can't get out of her own way. She is starting to do poorly in school and her attitude stinks. She is disrespectful, especially after her visits to you. She tells me that she doesn't want to go over there so often and would like to change the schedule to one night a week until 9 P.M. and every other weekend. I think that at the age of thirteen she should have some say in the plan.

I will be consulting with my attorney, and you will be hearing from us soon. Court seems to be the only thing that you listen to these days. See you there!

Jane

cc: Tom Jones, Esq.

As interactions such as those in the above letters continue to occur, you reach the end of your rope. "I'm just not going to bend anymore," you say. "I've been hurt enough. Every time I say yes, he/she takes advantage. I'm finished. No more Mr./s. Nice Guy/Gal." Unfortunately, it's quite likely that once again your ex feels the same way. In fact your interactions become contests. Who will win? Or, at least, who will not lose? "There's no way I'm going to be made a fool of this time," you think. You get used to this feeling, expect retaliation, get energized by the prospect of "winning," and get support from family, friends, and your attorney. This establishes the dynamic of *conflict addiction*.

Conflict addiction occurs when the battle becomes so important that it is almost impossible for one or both parents to behave in a manner that is best for the children (or at times even for themselves).

In essence, the conflict takes over. It becomes more powerful than the love of the children. It clouds thinking and impinges on the ability to make rational choices. On February 12, 2000, the *New York Times* reported a tragic incident when after what seemed like a high-conflict divorce, one parent reportedly called the other to inform him of the death of their son. The second parent hung up before the information could be conveyed!

Exercise: Are You Addicted?

Unfortunately, as with most addictions, the person addicted to conflict often doesn't realize it. Below is a short survey that can help you determine your level of conflict addiction.

Rate each item on a scale of 1 to 5. A 1 means the situation or feeling happens rarely to never. A 5 means it happens frequently.

_____ My ex argues with me over the silliest of things.

_____ Making decisions together with my ex is almost impossible.

_____ My ex almost always considers him/herself first, even over the children.

_____ Our children avoid talking about their other parent when they are with me.

_____ Our children have secrets from one or the other of us.

_____ Our children often do not want to see one of us.

_____ My ex and/or I often complain that we do not have enough information about the children.

_____ My ex and/or I complain that the other one is generally irresponsible.

_____ We continue to file legal motions over noncritical points that seem very important at the time.

_____ I would collaborate with my ex but he/she does not collaborate with me.

Now total the above 10 ratings. The lowest score you can have is 10, and the highest is 50. The higher your score, the more likely it is that conflict addiction is present. You may be sure that it is not your fault and that if your ex would behave everything would be fine. Yet the conflict continues. It consumes you, and worst of all, it consumes your children.

So, Why Can't You Stop?

Conflict is not what you feel. It is what you do. Popular thought suggests that conflict is caused by anger, feelings of superiority and the desire to intimidate, or feelings of inferiority and vulnerability. It is our opinion that "conflict" is best used to describe behaviors that people exhibit (rather than the feelings related to those behaviors). This is an extremely important concept that can help you have a more positive working relationship with your ex. Put simply, decreasing conflict is about what *you* do, not what you feel and experience. It certainly is not about what your ex does or does not do. This may be the most difficult concept for conflict-addicted parents to understand. If you view yourself as a victim of your ex, you will not focus on your ability to reduce conflict. Your view needs to be centered on *your* behavior and options, not those of your ex.

Many parents say they can't stop the conflict (even though they want to) because the other parent won't stop. Blaming each other keeps the conflict going. It keeps you feeling like the victim and as if you are not in control of your own actions. It's like children who say, "I did something wrong because [someone else] made me." The reasoning is, "I'm not to blame. It's [someone else's] fault, because he/she made me do it."

The conflict is also perpetuated by well-meaning friends and advisors (professional and otherwise). These individuals think they are helping when they say to you, "You can't let that happen. Your ex can't just get away with that. Here's what you should do." They are well-meaning instigators of conflict. It is easy for them to direct your life from their positions. But they aren't the ones who have to cope with the fallout of the conflict. They don't have to hear your children whimpering at night. They don't have to deal with your children's anger, or with the reaction of your ex, or with your sadness. Sometimes it is best to thank them for their input, briefly consider it, and then ignore it instead of crusading for what *they* think is best.

Sometimes the conflict addiction is so strong that parents actually fire their attorney for not being aggressive enough. Attorneys often tell us that they discourage excessive conflict. If that's not in line with what the parents think is best, the attorney may actually lose a client who wants to pursue a more aggressive stance.

In short, conflict addiction can be so strong that parents will go to extreme lengths, pay extreme amounts in legal fees, and go through extreme levels of discomfort to continue the conflict. The conflict, however, keeps alive the connection of the relationship. It is a justification for continued contact, and it provides an illusion of achieving justice or a resolution. It can be an attempt at some type of control. Unfortunately, it rarely if ever yields any of these outcomes on a permanent and healthy basis. Rather, it just keeps hurting (or destroying) you and your children. It destroys your objectivity and at times your ability to be at your best and care for your children. It destroys your ability to make decisions with the other person who truly is on your side. Yes, that's right: Your ex is on your side when it comes to your children. You both want what is best for your children. Parents who are in high conflict will all say with conviction that *they* want what is best for their children. They actually agree wholeheartedly with each other, even though they don't believe each other. Parents will fight endlessly for their children's sake. Conflict-addicted parents simply have the problem of fighting *against* each other *for* their children. They have the problem of viewing each other as the enemy.

CHAPTER 2

Conflict and Your Children

Your Children: The Last Connection

For couples who don't have children, the assets are distributed once the divorce is final, and then it's over. You can literally spend the rest of your lives without any contact. Children, however, are a family's most precious assets, and they cannot be divided up. Parents have to share them. Imagine the difficulty divorced adults would have simply sharing a joint checking account. We would say, "It's ludicrous to expect two divorced adults to share a checking account." Yet we are forced not only to share, but also to make joint decisions about our children. Children need and have a right to the love of both parents. They need access to and the influence of both parents. Frequently, they need both parents to collaborate in their upbringing. Children inevitably remain as the last connection between you and your ex. Even though the marriage is over, your relationship continues as parents who share in the lives of your children.

Imagine having a conflict-filled relationship with someone who cares for your children half of their lives. You would not tolerate hostility and disregard from your children's day care facility or from a housekeeper or nanny. You would dismiss them, change facilities, or in some way end the relationship. Unfortunately, you cannot fire your ex. They remain in place long after your children are out of the house. Why do the two of you tolerate the conflict in your relationship as parents?

The permanence of parenthood and the emotional connection we have with our children make us particularly vulnerable to becoming agitated. When we combine this with the hostility and hurt around a divorce, we can see why it is so difficult to avoid conflict. You both are heavily invested in your children. Unfortunately the conflict can cripple your ability to nurture and provide for those most precious gifts.

Levels of Conflict

Conflict is not an "on" or "off" phenomenon, and it is a typical aspect of most relationships. It comes from the push and pull of wills and personal agendas. It comes from old wounds and memories, from fear and loneliness, and from a loss of identity and dreams for the future. Conflict can even feel very self-protective and safe. When there is simply a disagreement, conflict is not problematic. However, as coercion begins and resistance escalates, the tug-of-war begins to develop. The tug-of-war leads to hostility and then serious conflict.

| Disagreement | Coercion | Hostility | Serious | Active Warfare |
| | Resistance | | Conflict | |

The Conflict Continuum

At its worst there is active warfare, which involves sabotage, spying, positioning, threats, and attacks. While these are terms of war, they occur between divorcing and divorced parents as well.

Stages of Conflict Development

In looking at your situation, you may find it useful to categorize the conflict level between you and your ex. Various authors (including Garrity and Baris 1994) have described the levels of parent conflict in different ways. Below are descriptions of different levels of conflict that we have found particularly useful. Determine which level best fits your general relationship with your ex. At times you may shift between levels, yet one level may describe your overall pattern.

Level I—Cooperation: Parents in Level I work together in the best interests of the children. They are able to be respectful of each other and make decisions. They do not fight over day-to-day issues and decisions. They try to understand each other's viewpoint and strive to make decisions relatively quickly and effectively. They rarely seek input from others on day-to-day matters. While they may have different parenting styles and different opinions about what is best, they do not try to dominate each other's parenting. They often give in to the other or compromise rather than fight.

Level II—Low conflict: These parents often disagree. They may bicker or squabble but do not let it get out of hand. They may briefly lose sight of the children's interests but then decide to refocus on the purpose of their interactions and on what is best for the children. These parents are able to listen to each other and attend to the needs of changing schedules and busy lives. They may keep some tallies of who did what and cautiously make agreements, taking an "I will if you will" approach. Making sure things are fair is important to these parents. These parents can sustain some flexibility and less structured parenting plans.

Level III—Moderate conflict: These parents are frequently in disagreement. They often position themselves in a way to either prove they're "right" or avoid being at a disadvantage. "I'm not going to let my ex get the better of me" may be the motto of the Level III parent. These parents often find themselves caught up in petty squabbles, which quickly get out of control. They may have good intentions but have difficulty turning these intentions into concrete reality. These parents may say, "You know, I called my spouse with a simple question. I just wanted to drop our child off a half hour later. I called and asked in a polite way, but the attitude I got back was unbelievable. Within minutes we were arguing about what happened last Thanksgiving. It's ridiculous. I don't know why my ex can't just stick to the topic at hand." Level III parents find it difficult to see their own individual role in the conflict. They try to coerce each other, resist being coerced, and will often be hostile with each other. These parents have difficulty being flexible and dealing collaboratively with new demands.

Level IV—High conflict: These parents are often in open warfare. They may be unable and unwilling to talk to each other. They may file countless legal motions. They may use their children to communicate information and have their children keep secrets from the other parent. They will often be accusatory and unwilling to bend. If they do talk, their speech is likely to be disrespectful and insulting. Sarcasm, condescending remarks, and profanity may be frequent occurrences. Cooperation is virtually nonexistent, and joint decisions are very difficult to make. Children may be informed of the failings of each parent, and each parent may be "sure" of the manipulative and impure motives of the other. Parents may take any negative information about the other and use it to their own advantage. Giving a child soup or cereal for dinner at 8 P.M. may be described as child neglect and as if that parent is putting the child at risk for being malnourished. A minor spanking may be regarded as child abuse. Allegations of sexual abuse may occur if a father gives his young daughter a bath. In short, these parents find it almost impossible to work together. They often turn to the courts to help them make basic decisions around parenting. They do not behave in a manner that fosters cooperation, effective planning, and collaboration in their parenting.

This book is applicable to parents at all levels. Level I and Level II parents may get some interesting new ideas that will help them be more flexible and responsive to the needs of their children. Level III parents may find they can contain the conflict they have and move into Level II more often. Level IV parents may find that this book can be an invaluable resource. It can give you ideas about how you can shift your behavior and break your addiction to conflict.

If you are a Level IV parent, you have probably given up hope. Your marriage ended but the battles did not. You may be convinced that nothing will ever change. As convinced as you may be, we have seen many Level IV parents make major changes to end the conflict addiction. Hope is important; however, your hope should be directed at yourself. *You can change your behavior*, even if you don't believe your ex can change. It's hard to have a war with one side. The less *you* battle, the less you will be addicted to the conflict.

Types of Conflict

Conflict addiction can occur in just a few or in many areas of the parenting relationship. Accurately assessing the types of conflict you have can go a long way to helping you focus your energies in an effective manner. If you know where and when you are most vulnerable to conflict, you can be vigilant and learn to change your approach. You can learn different strategies to apply to the situations where you are at the highest risk of conflict (i.e., where your addiction is strongest).

Decision Making

One of the most common places that conflict is evident is in the process of decision making. Parents can argue over the most trivial of differences between two alternatives. A major conflict can erupt over a fifteen-minute difference in pickup times or who gets to take the child to the new movie that has just been released. Parents argue over which parent should get to keep the trophy the child just won or what should happen to the family dog when the child goes to the other parent. When simple decisions become labor intensive, conflict addiction is likely.

Basic Values

Level IV parents often believe that their ex does not share the same basic values. You love your children. You want them to be healthy and happy. You want them to excel in their own unique ways based on their abilities, and you want them to have friends. You also believe that they should learn the difference between "right" and "wrong" and learn core values. High-conflict parents often assume that their ex does not hold the same beliefs. But why would only one parent want what is best for the child? In our experience with high-conflict parents, we find that they agree on values more often than they realize. They are just too busy disagreeing to notice. This fundamental misperception fuels the conflict. What's healthiest for your children is for you to assume that your ex has your children's best interests at heart. You are most likely to be correct in this assumption, believe it or not. Try not to assume that you need to protect your children from the other parent's beliefs.

The Exchange of Information

In war, information is coveted, held at a premium, and zealously defended. Spies are sent to get information from the other side. If they are discovered, they are tortured or shot—or both. High-conflict parents take a similar approach with information. They are resistant and at times refuse to share information about the children. They often stop associating with friends who are thought to "betray" them by sharing information with "the other side."

Without their knowledge, children are often the spies. They are exposed to information on both sides of the battlefield. Children are often sworn to secrecy. "Don't tell your father/mother . . ." At times, children are held captive by various techniques designed to obtain the secrets. They may be told, "It's okay to tell me, I'm your [parent]," or, more strongly, "I'm your [parent] and I'm asking you to tell me what your [other parent] did last night." Sometimes the approach can be more subtle and the child can be seduced or tricked into giving up the secret information. "You know, last night I was missing you. It was kinda late when I called and Suzi the babysitter picked up the phone. I guess [other parent] wasn't home. [Other parent] must have gone out with a friend, didn't he/she?"

Even medical information is sometimes withheld by parents addicted to conflict. "If you want to know what the asthma medicine is, you can call the doctor yourself. It's not my responsibility to tell you. You're a parent. Why don't you finally take responsibility to find out what your child needs instead of expecting me to find out and tell you just like I always did when we were married?" The cost of the conflict doesn't matter to conflict-addicted parents. When there is conflict addiction, the children are allowed to suffer. As with most addictions, maintaining the addiction becomes more important than its impact on you or those you love—your children.

Parent Alienation

Perhaps most devastating to children and their parents is the expression of conflict through parent alienation. When this occurs, we have a parent (or both parents) subtly or overtly denigrating the other parent in front of the children. "I can't believe your [other parent] did that. I just don't understand why or how anyone would do that." Some parents more subtly offer to support their child in his/her anger toward the other parent. "I understand that you're angry at [other parent]. I would be too, if [other parent] said that to me." They might then go on to support the child not seeing that parent. "I can certainly understand you saying that you don't want to see [other parent] tonight. If you want, I'll call him/her and say you want to stay here, especially given all the homework you have tonight."

Parent alienation is discussed in more detail in chapter 11. If you are concerned that you and your children may be a victim of this process, or that you may be accidentally supporting alienation, you are likely to be stuck in Level IV.

Organizing the Lives of Children

Sports practice, music or dance lessons, religious school, socializing, and homework are but a few of the many after-school demands on children. High-conflict parents have trouble with the coordination needed for these activities. At times, homework is not done when the children are at one parent's home. Children may have friends at one home but not the other. Coordinating around children's schedules becomes difficult for intact families. When there is high conflict in a divorced family, the conflict interferes with the organizational skills needed to address the many demands placed on the children and their parents.

Money ... Money ... Money

Oh yes, it's the money, isn't it? It always comes back to the money. Conflict-addicted parents are more than willing to argue over even a few dollars. They will spend thousands of dollars in legal expenses to battle over something costing far less. "It's the principle of the thing," they will say as a rationalization. "If I let him/her get away with this, I'll wind up giving in on everything." High-conflict parents will argue over who should pay for a ticket for the child for a recreational activity when one parent pays for the child's extracurricular activities in addition to, or as part of, the child support. Here, the money becomes more important than resolving the conflict or solving the problem. Parents have been known to argue over a tax bill for so long that the penalties and interest caused the total bill to double. As a divorced family, the conflict cost them double it otherwise should have.

If you are in Level IV, you can find countless opportunities to engage in conflict. Avoiding the conflict is difficult and often feels impossible. You may think the conflict is just between you and your ex, but you're wrong: The conflict most definitely involves your children. You may have heard the expression, "Anyone who attacks my children attacks me." The opposite is also true. "Anyone who attacks my parents attacks me." Each time two parents attack each other, they are attacking their children.

Children: The Victims of Conflict

Your children are the victims of the conflict between you and your ex. They're not the intended victims, but they invariably suffer from the conflict they witness—as well as the conflict they don't see. For example, conflict keeps parents from making decisions that are solely based on the children's interests. The conflict keeps parents angry with each other, leaving fewer emotional resources available for the children. It also occupies your attention, leaving less room for your children to get your attention. Isn't it amazing that the very person you divorced can get more of your attention than your children? Legal motions, phone calls, thinking about your next response to your ex's unreasonable demands and stances—these can all occupy your attention when you might otherwise be attending to your children.

Children of divorce have many common concerns, some of which are discussed below. We find that children of high conflict divorces may be even more likely than other children to have difficulty with some or all of these issues. It seems conflict serves as an amplifier, heightening the intensity of what children might experience if conflict were controlled.

Loyalty Issues

A child growing up in an intact family feels connected to both parents. In fact, families often talk about how "it's us against the world." Children often hear that *no matter what*, "we take care of each other" or "we are there for each other." The child is linked to each parent. The two most important people in the world are the child's mother and father. The child feels incredibly loyal to both. Then separation and divorce occur. If conflict is minimal this loyalty does not get shaken. But the very nature of highly conflictual relationships between parents stresses the child's loyalty.

You may have noticed during your divorce that it was difficult for you and your ex to stay friendly with your predivorce friends. Most of these people may have "chosen sides" or even stopped being friendly with both of you. Your children do not really have these options as they experience the conflict. They hear how either Mommy or Daddy is "good" or "bad," "fair" or "not fair," "generous" or "withholding," "mean" or "nice," etc. and are then put in the position of having to reconcile how they can love the parent who is "mean," "hurtful," "withholding," "unfair," or just "bad." This is further complicated by the fact that this "mean" parent is "mean" to the other parent (probably you). It would be bad enough if the parent were mean to a stranger, but in high-conflict divorces, one parent is attacking the other.

To make matters worse, the child also has to contend with the fact that there is one representation of who is "mean" when they are with one parent and naturally another representation of who is the "good guy" and who is the "bad guy" when they are with the other parent. So, when they are in your house, you're "great" and [other parent] is at fault. Yet, when they are with their [other parent], that parent is "great" and *you* are at fault. How much more confused and conflicted can your children become? The two people who have defined your children's values and their reality now define it in two distinctly different ways. Children are faced with the simultaneous dilemmas of, "How can I be loyal to Mommy, when Mommy is mean to Daddy?" and "How can I be loyal to Daddy, when Daddy is mean to Mommy?"

They also have to wrestle with the dilemma of trying to be loving to one parent when they know that this parent is, in essence, the "enemy" of the other parent. How can they fraternize with the enemy? Yet they are compelled by their love for you and your ex to stay in this impossible situation. Loving you both forces them to be disloyal to each of you at one time or another.

The act of being disloyal can create incredible anxiety. What happens in our culture when someone is disloyal? What happens when there is an act of betrayal or an act of treason? Your child might say to himself, "Look what happened to my mommy and daddy when one of them got so mad at the other one. What will happen to me if Mommy or Daddy gets mad at me?"

Abandonment Concerns

"Maybe Mommy or Daddy will leave *me*," is the natural answer to the above questions. "Maybe I will be left just like [one parent] was left. But if I'm left, who will take care of me? What if they both leave me? What will happen then? Who will take care of me then?" As adults, we know that we would never abandon our children, but children do not think as parents. They use a logic that is less cognitively mature. Their "logic" can easily be fueled by what they experience. The world around them proves them right or gives them new ways to understand what they experience. Your conflict supports their anxieties. It can recreate the divorce for them and bring up feelings similar to the separation anxiety they may have felt when they were toddlers.

How can we expect children to understand that what they hear parents say about the other parent does not apply to them?

"Mommy and Daddy don't love each other anymore."

"We're not talking to one another because when we do we fight."

"[Other parent] doesn't live with us because he/she loves someone else."

"Mommy and Daddy aren't married because [other parent] didn't try hard enough to work on our marriage."

It is easy for children to hear statements like the above as directly related to their own behavior and relationships with their parents. "If it can happen to Mommy and Daddy, it can happen to me. If they can leave each other, they can leave me."

The conflict between parents accentuates the anxiety about abandonment. It shows children that when the main relationships in their lives changed, people were unable to preserve the good parts of the relationship. It shows them that people who once loved each other are now on a crusade to fight with and hurt each other. You and your children may have lost hope. You and your ex may blame each other, and your children may blame themselves.

Self-Esteem and Self-Blame

Children often fantasize that they can keep mommy and daddy married. They believe that if they do the right thing, their parents might get back together. They believe that because *they* didn't do the right thing their parents divorced. Viewing themselves as the center of the universe they take responsibility for your actions. They take responsibility for the divorce and for the conflict. This can lead to a substantial decrease in self-esteem, self-confidence, and independence. It may affect the child's ability to form healthy adult relationships in the future (Wallerstein et al. 2000).

Children are also faced with their own feelings of anger and hurt toward their parents. This occurs in intact families too. However, when we add in the loyalty conflicts and fears of abandonment, we have children who can berate themselves for the situation itself as well as for what they feel about the situation. "I'm bad for being angry at my parents. Look at all they are going through. I shouldn't feel mad or cheated." Or, they might be saying, "I'm so bad. My [one parent] tells me my [other parent] is bad. But I love him/her. So, I must also be bad."

Parents Distracted by Conflict

Conflict addiction can be so seductive that parents continue to fight even as the children struggle with their own development. Some parents fight over which doctor their children should see rather than take them to the doctor. Others fight over the children's possessions to the degree that the children reject these items. Parents may be so antagonistic that transitions become difficult, stressful, and embarrassing to the children. Similarly, functions where the children would benefit by seeing both parents (e.g., school and academic events) are often disturbed by the conflict. Some children are embarrassed by being forced to take their clothes to school and then back and forth to each parent on transition days because the parents refuse to "leave the clothes *I* bought at [other parent's] house." High-conflict parents cannot routinely make effective choices that impact the health, safety, and security of their children without creating a disagreement. They lose sight of the children's basic needs.

As clinicians, we often think of the example of the child drowning in the middle of the lake when Mom and Dad are on the dock. Rather than jumping in, they are arguing over whose fault it is that the child is in the water. They argue over whether they should throw the life preserver to the child or swim out to him and who is better suited to rescue the child. As they argue . . . the child drowns!

Making Large Decisions Out of Small Ones

There are countless decisions to be made when raising a child. Parents without excessive conflict often make them without thinking. At times they simply say "oh well" and make the decision. At times they view the decision as just part of the general routine of raising a family. Unfortunately, conflict clouds the simplicity of garden-variety decisions. High conflict parents begin arguing over decisions in which they otherwise would have no interest. For example, they might argue over the selection of a scouting group. Or they argue over a fifteen-minute difference in bedtime. The arguing can actually keep them from initiating a change or having a common policy or procedure for the child. Instead, they complicate their lives and the lives of their children. They spend incredible energy on the power struggle. At times, they even return to court for a ruling. "We'll let the judge decide and then you'll see." A simple decision now goes to the court instead of to the parents.

Decreasing Flexibility

"You didn't bend when I asked, so forget it. You've got another thing coming if you think I'm going to bend for you." Most times, the flexibility doesn't benefit the other parent—it is actually for the children! The conflict again clouds this realization.

Naturally, the decrease in flexibility also affects both parents. High-conflict parents cannot easily deal with the inevitable "exceptions" to the routine. You cannot rely on each other when you are in a bind or when it would be more convenient. Let's say you just received tickets for you and the children to go to a show on Sunday afternoon. Unfortunately, it will be over at 5 P.M., which is when the children need to be home. You either need flexibility from the other parent or you miss the show, or you have to leave early so that you don't violate the parenting plan. If there is flexibility, you call the other parent and explain the situation. Unless there are some other major plans for Sunday evening, you are able to work this out because of the flexibility you have developed. Otherwise, you and the children are not fully able to enjoy the show and reap the rewards of this quality parenting time.

There are countless times when flexibility is important. This is one of the primary areas that high-conflict parents find is negatively and severely impacted by their interaction patterns. They keep track of how they were flexible and the other parent was not. They then reduce flexibility, claiming that they are going to teach the other parent a lesson. They have an ongoing feeling of resentment for the way their flexibility has been "abused" and for how the other has not reciprocated.

Many times, high-conflict parents actually do better when they settle down this process by going back to the parenting agreement without even trying to be flexible. Flexibility requires cooperation and understanding. If you are in the midst of conflict, this can be almost impossible. Returning to the specifics of the parenting plan can be a good idea but it is not likely to work if used as a threat or tactic when one parent wants control or to prove a point.

Modeling

"Do as I say, not as I do." Not surprisingly, this approach doesn't usually work. It certainly doesn't work well when it comes to the children learning from you how to deal with anger, disagreement, and differing needs. When children see their parents frequently battle over trivial things, speak in disrespectful tones to each other, and engage in hostile interactions, they too learn this manner of interacting. So, what happens when they are angry with you? To your surprise, they treat you with the disrespect they have witnessed. At these times many parents will comment, "My kids remind me of my ex."

Do your kids remind you of your ex or of yourself? Have they seen one or both of you engaging in behavior that you find reprehensible when it comes from your children? What will happen to them when they are in a relationship? Have you and your ex taught them that when a relationship "ends," what is left is perpetual bitterness and conflict? Have you taught them that love cannot be trusted? All they have to do to develop this belief is look at how it has ended for their parents.

Other Effects of Conflict

"Will you just stop yelling at each other?" the child pleads to her parents. "I hate you! All you do is fight with each other."

"I don't want either of you to come to my [game, school play, bar mitzvah, confirmation, graduation, or even wedding]. You two are impossible."

Conflict has also been shown to be a risk factor for later adjustment problems (Ellis 2000). Children who are victims of parental conflict generally have more difficulty with later adult adjustment than other children. If we think of childhood as a preparatory time for adulthood, we see that children learn many of the skills needed to negotiate the trials and tribulations of adulthood. Many of these skills relate to interpersonal relationships. The primary interpersonal relationship experienced by the children is that of their parents. This then becomes a major place where they learn the skills that prepare them to deal with other relationships in adulthood—with friends, employers, lovers, significant others, and their own children.

Conflict's effects are incredibly diverse. It is, in some respects, like a cancer as it attaches itself to the vital parts of your life. It strangles relationships and can sicken and kill even the healthy relationships in your life. Controlling conflict is possible. It first takes looking at the victims of the conflict: you and your children.

CHAPTER 3

Choosing the Children Over the Conflict

Looking Back

Think back to when your children were born. You can probably remember many of the details. You may recall the fears, the concerns, the pain, the joy, and the amazement. You may remember the feelings you had when you first held your baby, when you first took the baby home from the hospital, or when you felt that little hand grab yours for the first time. You may remember the warm feelings that came over you when you held your baby as it was sleeping. Or perhaps you remember the absolute panic that came over you when your child was ill for the first time.

When you decide to divorce, your focus shifts to your dying marriage. There are phone calls, endless documentation, and countless disputes. There are at least two attorneys involved. There may be even more attorneys if the children have an attorney and/or a guardian *ad litem*, or if one or both of you have changed attorneys. Every hour of legal time may cost $500 to $1000 total (depending on the number of attorneys). There are many hearings and court dates.

You probably feel or have felt many of the following emotions:

angry	hurt	frustrated	embarrassed
scared	enraged	depressed	overwhelmed

Can you still see your children through the morass of files? Can you see them through all the emotion and through the details of reorganizing and running your daily life? Can you see them through the conflict and the smoke that the battle leaves behind?

Your first inclination may be to say, "Of course, what are you talking about? I love my children. They're all I care about. I'm going through all of this for them." The following exercise will help you explore these feelings.

Exercise: Really See Your Children

Find a recent picture of each of your children. Study the photo(s) carefully. Look at your children's eyes. In a journal or on some spare paper, write a few sentences describing each of your children. Detail what makes them unique and special.

Next, write a few sentences describing what your children need most. What do you and your ex need to give them? In fact, if you and your ex could only give them three things, what would those three things be?

Did some of your answers include concepts related to love, happiness, and understanding of right and wrong, preparing them for adulthood, helping them with the special challenges they face (or you expect they will face)? If so, you are not alone. These are some of the core things that are important to parents—they're the overarching goals of parenthood (not soccer practice, grades, money, or prestige). These are what loving parents often look at as their primary responsibilities.

Who Loves Your Children?

Are you a loving parent? Do you love your children? Of course!

What do you think your ex would say to the same question? Do you believe your ex loves your children as well? If so, great! You're ready to start the journey toward decreasing the conflict. If you don't believe your ex loves your children, then you're at a disadvantage. This is a major concept that high-conflict parents need to address. If we asked your ex the same question, we might hear that he/she loves your children, but does not believe you do. Well, who's right?

We assume that parents who are in conflict love their children. They may not function in a way to win the "Parent of the Year" award, but they may truly love their children. In fact, love of the children is what keeps them in conflict. If they didn't love their children, we would likely see abandonment instead of conflict.

If you are going to have a chance of decreasing the conflict, you need to accept the possibility that you *both* love the children. If your ex has a copy of this book, you might want to compare what each of you wrote to the above two questions. You might be surprised at the similarity, even if the actual words are different.

More important is the question, who do your children love? Do they love just one of you? Do children need to be able to love and be loved by both parents? Except in the most extreme dangerous and abusive situations, they *do* need the love of both parents. They also need to be able to freely love both parents. If you hadn't gotten divorced, your children would love and be loved by both their parents. Why should this be taken away from your children as part of the divorce? Your divorce has already had a profound impact upon your children. Why should they also lose a parent (or two) because of the conflict in which their parents choose to engage? You may say, "It's not a choice." As we discussed in chapter 1, conflict is a set of behaviors. Your choice is whether or not to engage in these behaviors that inflict conflict on your children.

Who loves your children? You both do. Who do they need to be able to freely love? Both of you.

I Love My Kids More Than Anything

Of course you do. You say, "I would do anything for my kids. Anything." Yet parents who are addicted to conflict perpetuate the conflict at the expense of their children. A thirteen-year-old says, "My parents are enemies. They can't carry on a conversation without arguing." She feels distant from one parent and cries about it, saying she wishes she could feel closer. In this case love means that the parents need to put aside their anger toward each other in order to take care of their child. They need to love their child enough to stop fighting with each other and start showing their daughter that their feelings for her and their responsibility to her supersede the fighting. Parents in conflict need to put aside their resentment and distrust of each other (just like they used to put aside their fatigue for those feedings at 2 A.M.) to take care of their children. Loving your children means taking care of them "no matter what," and that includes setting aside conflict. It means not allowing the conflict to interfere with their care or their ability to get the best both parents have to offer. The marital unit may have dissolved, but the parental unit needs to be maintained no matter what.

Parents who overcome their conflict addiction are able to support each other. They are able to express their love for their children by supporting the children's relationship with the other parent and by supporting that other parent's attempt to build a healthy relationship with the children. They readily exchange information because the more they both know about their child, the better off their child will be. They focus on taking care of their most precious commodity—the children. They maintain a focus on the children and provide each other with information about the cognitive, emotional, and behavioral well-being of the children. They love their children in a way that concentrates their joint energies on providing for the well-being of the children.

Who Are Your Children With?

When your children are not with you (and not in school or daycare), who is with them? They're being cared for by their other parent. Right or wrong, collaboratively or not, consistently or not, that *is* where they belong.

If your parenting plan is 50/50, they spend six months a year in the care of someone else. If your ex has them every other weekend and one day during the week, they spend about 104 days a year (approximately three and one half months) with someone else. If you have them every other weekend and one day during the week, they spend approximately eight and one half months with someone else! Either way, the amount of time they are with your ex is considerable.

This person teaches them about life, sets limits, and provides rewards. This person cares for them when they are ill, helps them with their homework (or not), and comforts them when they need nurturance. This person also sets the stage for their growth and development and influences how they grow and thrive. How important is it for you to have a good—make that excellent—relationship with this person?

To look at it another way, imagine hiring a person to care for your children in your absence. You are going to be away from them for somewhere between three and nine months a year. This person will have full-time responsibility for the children. He/she will *not* have to follow your directives; they will be totally independent and able to make their own decisions and rules without having to check in with you. This person will be free to raise your children as *they* see fit. So, how important is it for you to have an *excellent* working relationship with this person? It is *crucial!*

It isn't just crucial for you. It's crucial for your children, because they pay the biggest price for your parental conflicts. If you were asked to choose between your ex and your children, the choice would be an easy one. You would of course choose the children. Yet, when asked to choose between the conflict with your ex and the children, the choice (while easy intellectually) becomes quite difficult from a day-to-day or behavioral perspective.

Choosing the children over the conflict allows you to solve problems and implement important changes in your children's lives. When you and your ex choose the children over the conflict, you can begin to jointly organize your children's lives. You can make decisions about doctors, schoolwork, extracurricular activities, changes in the parenting plan, etc. You can begin to communicate efficiently and effectively. You can support each other's efforts in parenting the children. You can learn from each other the strategies that seem to work best as parents. These can be strategies around discipline, toilet training, study skills, etc. You can give your children consistent messages about the values that you share. You can share in your children's development and future, even if you do not share a marriage. You can teach your children that parents can work as a unit, even if they are not married. You can teach them that parents who are divorced can still care enough to cooperate with each other and treat each other with respect.

Who Is Your "Ex," Anyway?

When you are divorced, your friends and family, the court, your attorney, and others refer to the person you were married to as your "ex." The relationship is defined by the marriage—or perhaps more accurately, by the divorce and the related conflict. The term "ex" is a reminder of the conflict and the failure of the marriage.

Thinking about your ex as "my ex" fosters conflict addiction. The term "my ex" first focuses on you. The word "my" makes it about you, not about your children. It orients the entire interaction around your own issues and feelings. The term "ex" doesn't relate to the role of the parent, but to the role of the spouse. While both of you are ex-spouses, neither of you is an ex-parent. Since the two of you are your children's parents, the term "parent" needs to be the central aspect of your role. Your job is to express your love for your children in a way that helps them develop and thrive. You help guide them, protect them, and teach them to survive in a healthy manner. Children need to feel the connection they have with their parents more than the connection the parents feel with each other. The primary relationship for children is with their parents as parents. It is not with their parents as spouses. Your roles as parents need to be emphasized and then emphasized again. You are not exes as far as your children's needs are concerned. You are parents. By referring to each other as "parents," you can continually orient yourself and each other to this crucial role instead of the hostility of the divorce.

You are *parents*, not exes, and you are certainly not "Mr." or "Ms.," as some parents tend to refer to each other.

How Much Information?

Let's begin with the scenario of two parents who live together. How much information do they need to exchange? Do they need to talk regularly? Do they need to collaborate in decisions? Do they need to support each other's decisions? Absolutely.

Does this change when parents are separated or divorced? Yes, it increases! The family system is more stressed, as are the parents and the children. They may even be somewhat disoriented by feeling that their world is turned upside down, or by loyalty conflicts or by the myriad other changes they experience as part of the divorce process. When life is calm and things are moving along smoothly, communication is not as critical. Conflict creates chaos, and in the midst of chaos communication becomes essential.

Exercise: Things You Need to Know

Let's go back to the example of having your children cared for exclusively by someone else for at least two months of the year. What would you want to know about this person and the care situation? In your journal or on your notepad, list some of the types of information you would need.

Next, list the information you would want the caretaker to have regarding your children.

Is this the information you and your children's other parent routinely exchange? Why not? If you say, "It's because my *ex* won't share this kind of information with me," you aren't beginning to change your behavior patterns and are simultaneously giving up control. Let's start over.

Saying "It's because my children's *other parent* won't share this kind of information with me" begins to shift your thoughts toward your parental roles. But this doesn't fix the problem of giving up control. The control becomes yours again when you decide that you will communicate with your children's other parent. If your children were with another caretaker for three months, you would give that caretaker plenty of information whether they asked for it or not. You would want them to have the information you wrote down while doing this exercise. You would begin by providing information because you know it's in your children's best interests. As one parent so aptly described it in today's lingo, "She has to download information to me to care for the children." This sets a tone for cooperation and the free exchange of information. If both parents take responsibility for providing information, the children have informed parents!

Protecting Your Children from Pain

Psychological and emotional pain is a part of life that we can't avoid. There are unfair situations and unavoidable traumas. Children get critically ill and parents die. Other children are mean to yours and some people behave in unscrupulous ways. Unavoidable pain befalls us from the outside. Most of the pain your children will experience will be outside your control, but the pain of conflict *is* under the control of both parents. Are you willing to protect your children from this pain? Should the pain associated with conflict be an exception?

Parents need to ask themselves, "What price should my children pay for the conflict I have with their other parent?" The only answer is $0; any other amount is too high and not their price to pay. Yet, all too often they do. What price do *your* children pay? Might they see your anger toward each other and the problems you have jointly caring for them as a sign that *you* don't love them enough? Might they think, "It is more important for my mommy and daddy to fight with each other than to take care of me?" They will carry these divorce issues with them well into adulthood. Wallerstein et al. (2000) interviewed children of divorce after twenty-five years and found a legacy of residual effects well into adulthood. Even children of low-conflict families will experience the effects of divorce as they begin to negotiate their adult relationships.

At best, children need their parents to parent them and to love them. They need to love their parents. Conflict addiction needs to be attacked with the same vigor that one might attack any other addiction; especially one that profoundly hurts your children. The fighting must stop.

CHAPTER 4

Conflict Resolution

Do You Love to Fight?

Parents who are addicted to conflict are so used to the angry feelings that they don't know how to function any other way. They may even feel exhilarated by the challenge of "winning" over the other parent. Their responses are instinctive and well entrenched. They are afraid to let go of the anger, and they find the antagonism usual and familiar. Their anger and attempts to have the last word are paramount. They truly lose sight of the best interests of the children as they act without thought and without taking a breath. These patterns are often well established and hard to break. Neither parent is ready to be the first to try to put aside the conflict. That feels far too scary!

When we're confronted, scared, confused, or angry, fighting is a very natural response. We observe this in research on the animal kingdom as well as in social psychology. Fleeing is the other usual reaction to upset, fear, and anger. Thus an approach/avoidance paradigm is established whereby an individual chooses one reaction or the other. Neither of these responses is a very effective co-parenting response. Children need parents who interact with each other.

Leave It to the Courts

Parents in high-conflict divorces are also used to going to court. They are used to spending much of their time in lawyers' offices, in courtrooms, and in therapy. The hope and expectation of each parent is that the judge will see their side. They know that they are justified and if only they could tell their story, then everyone will know who is right and who is wrong. They mistakenly believe that they want their day in court. The courtroom is seen as a place where one will have the opportunity to present the whole story. They can air all grievances and tell it all. Unfortunately, that kind of expulsive technique is not at all effective and only leaves everyone feeling angrier and drained of energy and finances. The courts are deciding issues from whether or not to sign children up for soccer, where to go to religious school, and who will provide sports uniforms, to more significant decisions about medical issues and schooling. These decisions belong back in the hands of parents. Who knows your children better: the judge, an attorney, a therapist, or their parents? The courts are more than happy to return children to their rightful owners—the parents.

Winning or Losing

When there is significant conflict, no one wins! The children certainly lose and so do the parents. If one parent prevails in court, no one has won. The conflict that ensued in getting there is not worth it. A parent may have a court decision that agrees with their proposal but what then? How does it get implemented? The aftermath of the battle is devastating and you need only listen to the children to understand their position. Uniformly, children want the fighting to stop. A dictatorship in parenting is the sound of only one voice talking. Children of divorce have their best chance when two parents learn to work together. Parents need to stop saying "I'll see you in court."

When parents engage in significant conflict, they expend enormous amounts of energy battling with each other. This is surely energy that could be better spent on their new lives. The old issues with an ex can continue to take up large amounts of time and refocus a parent on the marital disagreements and communication difficulties. The children become the victims once again. If one parent is hurt, humiliated, or subdued by the other parent, then the children are subsequently hurt as well. Children will often rush to defend the hurt parent or if scared, they will rush to join the attacking parent. Neither one of these options promotes a healthy adjustment to the divorce. Fights, arguments, and sarcastic and condescending tones rarely, if ever, solve a problem.

High-Conflict Communication

Parents who engage in significant conflict have their own language. They love to talk *at* the other parent. They do not know the meaning of the word "listen." Their conversations are often either like that of little school-age children or more sophisticated and cynical like adolescents. For example:

- They use lots of derogatory terms: name-calling, labeling, cursing, etc.

- They use lots of accusatory statements.

- They love to play the "gotcha" game or get the last word.

- They love to threaten (especially to say "I'll see you in court.").

- They love to test the other parent or play the "Do you really love the children" game.

None of these techniques are in the best interests of the children. The basic premise of all of the above is that the other parent is not good for the children and/or that not having to deal with the other parent would make everyone's lives a lot easier. But the children only lose. They learn a lot about conflictual communication but not a lot about conflict resolution. They do not learn how to deal with their own anger or how to collaborate with someone whom they do not choose as a partner either at home or at work. They too become skilled at conflict because they have the best examples in the world—their parents.

Behaviors That Prohibit Cooperative Communication

Filibustering

When parents engage in conflictual communication, they talk instead of listen. The point of the interaction is usually just to state their position. They don't even notice if someone else is really listening. They listen to themselves and talk for the sole sake of getting something said but with no real intention of attempting a resolution. Of course, they expect to leave that up to their lawyers and the courts. They aren't really taking responsibility for their children; filibustering is for their own needs and certainly not those of their children. They have the floor and they do not want to give it up. The purpose of a filibuster is usually to prevent anyone else from having the opportunity to speak. It uses up time and it wears down the other side. It is great theatre.

All those words and all that emotion make the speaker believe even more strongly in his or her position. In high-conflict relationships, each side truly believes they are right. They work to convince the other parent. They almost *never* believe that the other parent might have something useful to say about their children.

Mind Reading

Parents in high-conflict divorces avoid talking and communicating as much as possible. Yet they expect the other parent to have all the information necessary to make decisions, show up at events and activities, and make appropriate disciplinary choices. And then they say, "I know what you mean by that" and "I know why you did that."

In most situations, we don't expect other people to read our minds. Why should we expect parents with poor communication and hostility to be successful at mind reading? Parents need to exchange ideas, facts, and observations in order to carry out the business of co-parenting. Remember the old Johnny Carson game on the *Tonight Show*, the Amazing Karnak? Did you get the questions right most of the time or are those odds pretty poor? Single parenting is hard enough. Don't make it tougher by playing the mind-reading game.

Nonverbal Signals

There are numerous ways to communicate. One of these is the powerful means of nonverbal communication. Children are masters of assessing nonverbal cues. Babies will cry when held by someone who is uncomfortable holding them, and will become restless upon sensing the tension of the adults around them. Adults can tell immediately when they have intruded on a tense discussion. Children are also very used to picking up on these same nonverbal signals with their friends and parents.

Nonverbal cues that were a source of friction during the marriage can unfortunately still be a problem and a trigger for antagonism. Remember how he/she used to roll their eyes, wave their hand, tap their fingers, swing their leg, give the thumbs-up or thumbs-down? These behaviors remain infuriating and can reinitiate the conflict in an instant. Parents need to be aware of their behavior just as they would if working with a business partner. They also need to avoid being distracted by the other parent's hostile nonverbal behavior as this distraction leads to mind reading and detracts from solving problems and reaching decisions in an efficient manner.

Unilateral Decision Making

Is it really an emergency or can it wait? Co-parenting requires that each parent consult the other parent when making any significant decisions. Parents who are addicted to conflict often act as if each decision is a crisis. They often seek and then take the opportunity to make unilateral decisions. In this way they avoid the expected conflict with the other parent. They believe that any discussion will lead to an argument and a stalemate. They do not deal with their ex and instead take the faster, easier route—they just decide for themselves. Of course an explosion often occurs, a better decision may be missed, and more conflict is fostered. It would seem that after this occurs repeatedly, a parent could predict this pattern and outcome. Once again we have evidence of the intense addiction to conflict that warring parents can possess. If the negative result is to be expected, then why do it? If what you do doesn't work, why do it? Maybe you are used to the feeling and familiarity of intense conflict. Change can be scary and difficult.

Fear of Silence

Peace and quiet is not the norm for high-conflict parents. They are used to the intensity of the attorneys' offices or the courts. Respectful and calm communications are not the ordinary means of interaction. Even when the communication begins to become less hostile for a time, high-conflict parents usually return to their loud, antagonistic, and conflict-perpetuating behaviors. Another motion is filed, an attorney is consulted, another letter is sent, e-mails fly, faxes arrive, voice mails and messages are left. These one-sided communications are extremely frustrating for the other parent and will most often be met with escalation and vigorous retaliation. Rather than learning to work together, they spend more money and waste more time. The children suffer in the interim as they watch, hear, and feel their parents reengage in the parenting battle.

The real underlying feeling that most parents reexperience is fear. As one parent so poignantly put it in a parenting session, "I'm afraid that this just might work. Then we would be able to do this parenting thing together. But that is what I wanted to happen while we were married, so this would feel very sad." That is truly the hard reality for co-parents after a divorce. Once the fighting stops, the job of working together really begins. They just might be able to accomplish it better apart than together. For high-conflict parents, it's the fact that they're no longer together that opens up avenues for them to communicate and co-parent effectively.

Promoting Cooperative Communication

There are a number of skills that promote cooperative communication: anger management, listening, and conflict resolution strategies. These techniques need to be learned and applied in a very determined manner. Parents need to prepare, plan, and implement well-practiced behaviors so that they stop reacting from instinct and impulse. It is hard to remember how to control your emotions when you are in a situation with someone who knows so very well how to push your emotional reaction buttons. High-conflict parents have spent much time learning the art of "button pushing." They need to spend a considerable amount of time and energy being mindful when using their new nonconfrontational behaviors.

Understanding and Managing Anger

Anger after a divorce is a common reaction to feeling attacked or to a situation that feels out of control. Anger is a very typical response but it often results in feelings of greater powerlessness. It rarely gets long-lasting, positive results. It can be destructive to a relationship when expressed in an unbridled and uncontrolled manner. The expression of anger and hostility does little to garner respect and cooperation. Do you listen when sprayed with anger? Do others listen when you spray anger? There are a number of ways that anger is handled:

Anger can be expressed as hostility or aggressiveness. The goal here is to get the other person to do what you want through force and intimidation; for example, launching a direct verbal attack or accusing the other parent of neglectful or hurtful behavior toward the children. Force begets force. If you strike out, you should expect retaliation, which may happen now or when you least expect it.

Anger can be kept inside. The goal here is to avoid the feelings, but they are likely to appear in other ways, such as filing motions for contempt or changes in custody without notifying the other parent. Feelings that are stuffed inside often simmer until they boil over.

Anger can be expressed indirectly through behavior. The goal here is to interfere with situations so that the other person is inconvenienced and is annoyed by the behavior. For example, passive-aggressive behaviors such as consistently being late or forgetful are indirect expressions of anger and hostility. Hostility leads to retaliation and escalation of the conflict.

Anger can be translated into assertive communication. The goal here is to reach a conclusion and effect a resolution of the problem. For example, assertive communication involves a parent attempting to calmly discuss the issues and devise a plan of action with the other parent.

Obviously, the fourth option is the best way to express angry feelings. Unfortunately, it requires much forethought, practice, and concentration. When parents are in the throes of a discussion and it is not going the way one of them wants, it is hard to drop back and try to implement strategies that could possibly save the exchange from being aborted.

The following are more specific ways in which parents can prevent their anger from getting in the way of solving problems and reaching conclusions.

Take Your Time

Angry responses are often impulsive and usually indicate that you aren't listening to yourself. Many high-conflict parents sound like angry adolescents. They need to know NOW! Everything is treated as an emergency, even when it is not. Try not to decide the more important issues immediately. Think about your feelings, pick your battles, listen to all sides, formulate your opinion, and then devise a reasonable solution to the problem.

Listen, Listen, Listen

High-conflict parents like to talk, but they hate to really listen. Listening might mean that they will not get their way. They interrupt, and they are rude and disrespectful. This type of behavior would never be tolerated in any business setting or if engaged in by the other parent. If you would like to be heard, then you will have to do your share of listening. Behaving as an "adult" will promote more opportunities for conflict resolution.

Can I Finish PLEASE?

High-conflict parents do not let each other finish a thought. This may come from years of interacting in which they probably tolerated this type of marital exchange. You cannot know what the other parent is thinking if you don't give them a chance to get a word in edgewise. They just might have a point or might even be agreeing with you. You wouldn't want to miss that! And yes, they just might know what is best for your children too.

Let's Talk Nicely

High-conflict parents often lack rules when they are conversing with one another. They feel that they can say just about anything they want in any way that they want. When interacting with others in our lives we would never speak to them in such derogatory terms. We have enough respect for the relationship to avoid doing that. This type of conversation accomplishes nothing and is usually not even very satisfying. Talking nicely to one another is essential to the process of listening. Do not use contemptuous and sarcastic remarks or blaming, even if you feel like it. In fact, imagine that your interactions are to be videotaped and played to your children. You should be proud of, not embarrassed by, your behavior.

The Past Is the Past

It is not helpful for high-conflict parents to rehash old issues and old hurts. The job after divorce is to parent the children and not to resolve the former marital issues. If that could have been done, then you would not have sought a solution through divorce. When high-conflict parents try to talk about their old history as a couple, they usually end up fighting and then not solving the issues at hand today or in the future.

Keep It Short

Communications that are too lengthy are frequently not heard. Additionally, long conversations leave too much time for you to get into trouble. It isn't always important to share all of your feelings on an issue. High-conflict parents are hypervigilant and sensitive, so they pick up on every nuance. The more they talk, the more chance there is to misinterpret, misspeak, and feel hurt, neglected, or attacked. The more talk, the more chance there is to get into trouble!

Relax

Each of you is responsible for your own emotions. If you don't want the interaction to be fraught with anger, then prepare yourself well. Stress-management techniques work to lower heart rate, lower blood pressure, and reduce the impulse to respond emotionally. High-conflict parents are always on guard against any possible transgression or assault. Therefore they are always in a ready position, poised for action or poised for a fight. The implementation of relaxation exercises can help you approach parent communications with less tension and animosity. Besides that, they make you feel better too!

Effective Communication

While it seems that communication is an objective process, it is actually quite subjective. Many times, the messages that are sent are distorted. You may find that your comments "come out wrong" or are misheard by others. At times our own perceptions and biases distort the messages that are sent to us. Additionally, nonverbal behavior greatly affects the way that conversations are interpreted. High levels of distress, anger, and conflict can further distort people's messages. While children need their parents to communicate with each other clearly and effectively, high-conflict parents often exchange communications that are unclear and send many mixed messages. Here are some helpful hints.

Keep it simple. It is often helpful to communicate using short sentences with specific messages. As the sentences become more complicated, it is more likely that you'll be misunderstood and communication will falter.

Focus on your communication goals. It is important to be clear about the messages you want to communicate. Concentrating on just one, two, or three goals of the communication can help you avoid getting sidetracked into useless discussions and possible arguments. Staying focused can lead to efficient and succinct interactions.

Seek to understand. Spend more time focused on understanding the other parent's point of view or central message. If you truly understand the message they are intending to state, you can effectively respond. Remember, they love your children too and just might have a good idea.

When in doubt, check it out. It is crucial to be certain that you truly understand the messages you receive, and that the other parent correctly understands the messages you are intending to send. Taking the time to make sure you "get it" before going on is quite beneficial. High-conflict parents rarely ask for clarification. They just assume that they know what the other parent means. They love to mind-read, and given the history of relationship problems, they are often incorrect.

Pay attention to your own nonverbal communication. Body posture, tone of voice, and eye contact are all important nonverbal factors that influence communication. If you exhibit hostility or disregard, this is likely to cause a negative reaction and contribute to the deterioration of the communication process. On the other hand, communication behaviors that demonstrate caring for the children and regard for the other parent can help facilitate communication. Many high-conflict parents sit with their arms crossed, make little to no eye contact, point fingers at each other, get in each other's face, hang up the phone abruptly, and even make dramatic exits to make their point.

The only point this behavior makes is that they want to win and are not truly focused on taking their children's best interests to heart. They also are not behaving in a manner that breeds respect and cooperation.

Resolving the Conflict

We have already mentioned that parental conflict is the highest risk factor for children's poor adjustment to divorce. It is so easy to engage in conflict—but it is also easy to resolve conflict if each party is personally willing to take responsibility. Unfortunately, parents who are engaging in conflictual communication often expect the other person to change the pattern. High-conflict parents are afraid to go first, for several reasons: They fear that the other parent won't play fair and they will be making themselves vulnerable to attack or to being taken advantage of. They expect deceit, and they expect their communications to be contested. It's like the old Mexican hat dance, where one dances around the edge of the hat very gingerly and carefully. Neither parent can trust the other one enough not to hurt them. They don't believe that the other parent truly understands what is in their children's best interests.

When we ask parents to co-parent after a divorce, we are asking them to do something that can seem impossible. We ask them to create an environment that is as conflict-free as possible. We ask them to conduct the complicated logistics of children's lives: schedules, homework, equipment, appointments, etc. We ask them to partner with someone with whom they had a romantic relationship that failed. We ask them to talk to that person regularly. We ask them to make decisions with someone with whom they may differ in ethics, values, and other major areas. We ask them to consider the other parent as their consultant. We ask them to keep each other up to date and well informed. We ask them to work together to create a life for the children that allows them to grow up as children and not be burdened with adult issues and concerns. We ask them to make their "enemy" their ally. *That* is what is in the best interests of the children.

Guidelines for Effective Communication

The following guidelines are offered as practical advice that can be helpful in reducing conflict in communications between high-conflict parents:

Communicate with your children's other parent because you love your children and care about their future. A major point to keep in the front of your mind is that *your children need you both*. You must learn to work together. Otherwise, you run the terrible risk of subjecting your children to potential effects that could create lifelong difficulties. You are their examples of how people who do not choose to be together can find ways to accomplish their goals in spite of their differences. This is a valuable lesson that they can take with them into all aspects of their lives. Don't try to win. Try to solve.

Seek to make sure that you understand the purpose of the communication. The goal of communication about the children is to simplify their lives, solve problems, and make the adjustment to the ongoing stress of divorce as easy as possible. You and the other parent have a common purpose or a common problem to be solved. Be sure not to allow your interactions to become opportunities to veer off task and stray into old areas that will only lead to conflict and not to resolution. Stop the exchange at that time rather than continuing on until there is a heated debate and the conversation tone changes into an accusatory yelling match.

Keep your ego out of it. Communication between parents should not be based on your own self-esteem. You and your old relationship issues are not what matters now. It is the children whose interests must be addressed. Sometimes what is best for them is not always your way. It may inconvenience you, it may seem unfair, or it may even mean that you miss some of your parenting time with them. Married or divorced makes no difference here. Do what your children need and not what you want.

Don't argue. Arguing rarely solves a disagreement. It is quite unlikely that in the midst of the argument one of you will turn to the other and say, "Gee, now that you put it that way, I fully and whole-heartedly agree." Arguing changes the purpose of the communication and gets you nowhere fast. Try to get the conversation back on track by taking these three steps: recognizing the deviation in communication, stopping, and restarting the exchange. It's like pushing the restart button on your computer to reboot. Sometimes it can be helpful to set a time to talk about it later, when you're both calmer or in a better position to come up with a solution.

Avoid remarks that are provocative in nature. Hurling bitter insults, yelling, and rolling your eyes does little to resolve conflict. Once you begin to engage in this behavior you are heading down the slippery slope to disaster. It may feel liberating for the moment to call your children's other parent every name in the book, but in the long run you have only caused a major setback in the parental relationship, from which it will be difficult to recover. Each time this happens it makes it even harder to recoup your losses. This was true during the marriage and remains true afterward as well. The most common provocative remarks are challenges to trust, reliability, character, caretaking skills, honesty, and the children's view of their relationship with the other parent.

Politely terminate conflictual interactions. You always have the chance to STOP and try again when communications turn sour. If conflict cannot be easily resolved, it is often better to postpone future discussion to a later time rather than to try to prove your point. You can use the hold button for any interaction. Take a breath and start again, or make plans to reschedule. Simply tell the other parent that you need to continue this at another time, and tell them what time works for you. Do not hang up, slam a door, stomp away, or demonstrate other angry behaviors. Remember that you are the role models for your children's future relationships.

Apologize freely. If there is a misunderstanding and conflict escalates, the cost of the interaction increases. It costs nothing to apologize for a behavioral or communication error. Such an apology can serve to rapidly de-escalate the situation and avoid excessive damage. It is like pulling the fuse out of a stick of dynamite. Apologies can bring surprisingly favorable responses. The other parent can begin to trust that you do have the children's best interests at heart. The other parent can see that you are paying attention to your communications, and can clearly see that you can manage your own anger and change the interaction. The other parent might just imitate you in the future.

Look for something you can agree upon. Agreeing on what is in your children's best interests is much more productive than disagreeing over your individual opinions. Seek to find some common ground from which to work toward resolution. High-conflict parents are often so busy disagreeing for the sake of disagreeing that they don't even recognize that they are really on the same side. They delay finding a solution even when the easy answer is staring them in the face. It again feels like a "loss" to agree with the other parent. For instance, parents may be arguing over whether or not their child should play hockey. They may agree that the child should play the sport, but then have trouble with the transportation logistics. The child will lose out if they don't realize this quickly. Stop and identify the areas of commonality before tackling the implementation issues.

Search for a partial solution. Partial solutions can be much more useful than arguing over the "perfect" solution. Partial solutions can also lead to creative alternatives that neither parent may have wholly considered. The old saying "You can't always see the forest for the trees" applies here. High-conflict parents get hooked on their own way of viewing things and cannot always see that there may be other viewpoints. Of course, they certainly do not want to see that other viewpoint come from the other parent. There are usually a number of possibilities that can work, but if it feels like you are "giving in" to the other parent, you are more likely to hold fast and not brainstorm other options. High-conflict parents get stubborn and narrow-minded, a level of cognition analogous to that of a young child. Anger and hurt can cause amazing levels of regression even in the highest-functioning adults. Stay in an adult mode and you maintain control.

Get another opinion. There are a number of resources to which parents can turn when they are locked in high-conflict battles. Individual attorneys can be helpful, but remember that they are there to represent you. They may advise you in ways that sometimes can inflate the parental conflict, because they are acting in *your* best interests. Attorneys for the minor children represent your children's interests. If your children are older, this may mean that the attorney speaks for them. Attorneys are excellent resources for an alternative voice and can sometimes tell you things that you may not be able to hear from the other parent or even from the children themselves. Guardians *ad litem* are appointed to act in the best interests of the children. They are supposed to see the forest for the trees, when the parents cannot. They can often cut through the conflict to do what is necessary for the sake of the children. They are another wonderful resource with whom to consult when the conflict level supersedes the parents' abilities to resolve differences and make decisions. These resources are related to the legal system and take the control out of the hands of parents.

The courts are making all sorts of decisions these days that should really belong to you—and it's certainly not the court's preference. The court is forced into this role by the battling between parents. Someone has to take charge of an out-of-control situation. Major medical decisions may have to be made, or perhaps the children deserve to take a vacation with the other parent. When the court gets involved, the responsibility shifts, so high-conflict parents can then say that it was the court's decision and not theirs. Some states are now requiring divorcing parents to participate in mandatory parent education classes. These classes vary in length, format, and size. They provide a wealth of information to a group of parents but cannot address the individual needs of various couples. High-conflict parents can learn a lot from these kinds of classes but often go home just to reengage in the war all over again. They may need something that's much more individualized.

Another resource is forensic parent counseling. Programs such as our P.E.A.C.E. (Parents Equally Allied to Co-Parent Effectively) program provide structured intervention for parents engaged in patterns of high conflict. These types of programs are designed to put the control back into the hands of parents and relieve them of their reliance on the court to solve their parenting problems. It requests that parents and their attorneys agree that there will *not* be any further litigation while the parents are engaged in this counseling process. The goal is to directly teach skills that will help parents resolve differences and not reengage in old issues. It gives parents the opportunity to work together without their attorneys involved but also works closely with the attorneys to keep everyone well informed and well aware of the parents' progress. This can be a successful alternative to motion after motion or to custody evaluations, which may develop a reasonable parenting plan but cannot teach the parents how to implement the specifics. Plans and evaluations can provide the structure for parenting but not the methods for carrying out the specifics. This approach is not psychotherapy oriented. It is highly directive and solution oriented and not aimed at resolving the old marital issues. Rather, it focuses on developing the parents' abilities to work together in the best interests of their children.

Most parents view themselves as good parents to their children, and most high-conflict parents do not think very highly of the other parent. But even if they cannot find fault with the parenting style and parent/child interactions of the other parent, they still are reluctant to support each other in front of the children. The children grow to believe that conflict should be preserved at all costs. They learn that mistakes are not just mistakes but rather deliberate insults and manipulations. The life lessons they learn are not at all healthy or hopeful. The children may even end up learning how to help preserve the conflict as they try to please both parents. Parents may generally view themselves as warm and kind individuals in most of the rest of their lives. Yet in the presence of the children's other parent they can become nothing less than a "monster."

You can control this behavior, and you can avoid allowing the other person to provoke you. You don't have to be a victim of his or her behavior. Rather, you can take charge of your own behavior, change the tone of your parent interactions, and show your children how adults can effectively manage their emotions, express their feelings, and resolve their conflicts.

CHAPTER 5

Building a Co-Parenting Relationship

What Is a Good Co-Parent?

Co-parenting after a divorce (or if you were never married) is a very difficult job. Do not underestimate the amount of effort and attention it takes to establish a setup that works. The key lies in recognizing that you have to work together! The skills described in the previous chapter are essential in this process. You need to listen, articulate, compromise, and make decisions in a timely manner. Successful co-parents try their best to keep their children's interests first and foremost. Difficult though it may be, they make every effort not to shift the focus to their own needs or their anger and desire to retaliate. High-conflict parents have an even harder time following these principles because they assume that the other parent is the problem. They fail to take a hard look at their own commitment to the co-parenting relationship. They shift so easily into a conflict mode that they don't even notice that the tone and quality of their interactions have changed. They get in too deep before they can pull back from the slippery slope of hostility. Successful co-parenting requires flexibility and a sincere recognition that parental conflict is destructive to your children's future. If you intend to follow a shared parenting plan, you must be dedicated to the concept that the children need you both.

Determination and perseverance are two important basic traits that foster success. Even if high-conflict parents have these attributes, they may fail to effectively apply them. Co-parenting is hard work, and high-conflict parents are all too ready to give up. No matter how long it took to get their relationship into this hostile state, they want instant success and proclaim the failure of any attempt that does not work right away. They have very little patience and are quick to point out the misbehavior of the other parent while ignoring or minimizing their own violations. Establishing a good working co-parenting relationship takes time. Gains for high-conflict parents are initially small and must be measured in different ways. High-conflict parents tend to use yardsticks that are much too ambitious for them (or even for parents in intact marriages). Successful co-parenting can be assessed by:

- Less litigation and attorney involvement

- Cordiality and civility in parent interactions

- Regular nonconflictual communications

- An ability to attend children's events and activities together without overt hostility

- Cooperative decision making on essential issues

- Cooperative decision making on most routine issues

- Flexibility in changing plans

- Support and help for the other parent when needed

While we've emphasized that you shouldn't rehash your marital problems with you ex, it's still important that you as an individual deal with the divorce aftermath. Co-parenting cannot be successful if you haven't adequately dealt with your own issues concerning the demise of your marriage. Individual or group psychotherapy or counseling may be necessary to accomplish this goal. Otherwise, old hurts and anger can interfere with the process, causing emotions to take over when rationality is needed. Good co-parenting is an exercise in being reasonable. Imagine expecting the other parent, whom you assume is never going to change, to listen with a dedication to joint decision making. Now even more important, imagine that for yourself. You aren't perfect either! You have to actively, positively, and reliably contribute to the process.

The Business of Co-Parenting

Much of the literature on co-parenting after divorce discusses the idea of forming a business relationship dedicated to decision making around the children (e.g., Ricci 1980). High-conflict parents especially need to try interacting this way. However, they need a different focus and a different structure. Co-parenting for these parents is not a business relationship between willing partners who value each other and look to each other for an opinion. Most business partners expect each other to complete their part of a task in a timely manner and to follow through with their assignments and agreements. This isn't the case with high conflict parents. Instead, it is more like a business relationship with a partner whom you do not trust, would not select voluntarily, would like to fire, and with whom you often disagree. This business relationship can be quite volatile and openly hostile. High-conflict parent partners do not keep their promises, profess to be focused on the same goal but instead act in completely different ways, delay, take stands just to disagree, try to control tasks in a determined manner, do not show up on time, get the schedule time confused, change the plans or decisions in mid-stream, withhold information, lie, make derogatory comments, act condescending, etc. Given the above, who in their right mind would choose to work with someone like that? The fact is that you don't have a choice. You are parents, together and you can't eliminate the other parent from your children's lives. It's essential that you find a way to work together to raise your children in the best way possible.

Many high-conflict parents need strictly predetermined ways of interacting to make their business relationship work on a regular basis. The goals of establishing this kind of structure are efficiency and effectiveness. The work must be completed without overt hostility and it should never involve the children.

The Parenting Phone Call

High-conflict parents need a scheduled means of interacting with each other to conduct their parenting business. One useful strategy is to have a weekly parenting call during which you discuss a regular agenda and make the decisions needed to parent the children. This call limits other interactions and replaces all those intermittent calls received at inconvenient times. Most issues can really wait for this call. A weekly call is recommended, with any other interactions limited to emergencies or other business that absolutely cannot wait. This parenting business call should not be conducted in front of the children and should be given a regular and appropriate time and place to ensure its success.

Scheduling the Call

The parenting call is usually held once a week at a routine and mutually convenient time. The parent who is caring for the children at the time of the call should place the call. This assures that the children are in bed or at least out of earshot of the exchange. In this way the children are protected from the possibility of overhearing any parental conflict. Most parents pick an evening time, but some parents prefer a weekend morning or even a weekday at work during a break or lunch hour. Remember that this call is a planned meeting time and should be treated with the same respect that you would treat any scheduled business meeting. You should prepare in advance, show up on time, reschedule if you cannot make it, be prepared to work, and expect to solve the problems at hand. If one parent cannot make the call at the scheduled time, then it is his or her responsibility to notify the other parent (preferably in advance) and find another mutually agreeable time to complete the call. It is important to give each other ten minutes of leeway in being late for the call. If the parent receiving the call does not answer, the caller should leave a message and call back in ten minutes. At the second attempt, the parent calling should leave another message, but it is not necessary to keep trying to call after that. It is the other parent's turn to call back. By the way, all parents need answering machines or voice mail. Many even have caller ID so they know who is calling. Answer the phone!

The Agenda

Because parenting phone calls are just like business meetings, they should have a planned agenda. Most of the agenda items are discussed each week, sometimes very briefly and sometimes in much greater detail. Other items are discussed cyclically and still others are only discussed once in a while. The key to a successful parenting agenda is preparation. Just as you would think about and perhaps write down your thoughts prior to your business meeting, you need to do the same for your parenting phone call. It isn't fair to say to the other parent, "I haven't really thought about that," when the agenda items are well defined for both of you. Would you tell your business partner that you had not really considered the issues beforehand? That would certainly convey disinterest, disrespect, and even arrogance. If the goal of the call is to upset the parenting relationship and not to make any decisions, then it is easy to do just that. But if the goal is to make some mutual decisions and to discuss the children's lives and welfare, then you need to formulate your ideas well ahead of time. It is advisable to write down your thoughts in an informal way so that the emotions that may be expressed do not get in the way of solving the issues or even just discussing the various interesting details and events in the lives of your children.

The following is a sample agenda, which of course needs to be modified depending upon the age and developmental level of the children.

The Good Stuff: Imagine getting parenting phone calls that begin with a positive tone and good news. How would you feel, compared to receiving calls that start with another "problem" to discuss or with criticism? Try starting your calls with "good stuff." Remember that you aren't with your children at all times. When the other parent is with the children, they continue to go about their lives and do all those cute and wonderful things that make their childhood so memorable. If you don't communicate with the other parent regularly, you'll miss out on all those moments. The parenting call is an excellent opportunity to share the good stuff. One wise attorney suggested that parents begin their phone call with this section. In this way, they establish a positive tone for the conversation, which is far more conducive to compromise and sharing. In short, convey all the information you would want to receive. In this case, more information is better than less.

Medical issues: Discuss current illnesses, upcoming and recent doctor appointments, dental appointments, medication requirements, and information about any chronic conditions.

School related issues: Academic performance, behavior in school, homework, conference schedules, teacher comments, and other school events (concerts, meetings, plays, performances, athletics) can be discussed here. Many times both parents are already getting some of this information, but all too often notices go only to one parent. Children also tend to notify one parent of all those little unscheduled times that parents are expected to be involved in school functions. Convey this information to each other so that your child or the school personnel does not have to ask, "Where is Dad or Mom?"

Activities: Children these days are often involved in many different activities, and the logistics alone can be mind-boggling. Parent coordination is essential, but for divorced parents the scheduling is even harder. Every week it is important to check out the week's schedule with each other. Who is driving whom where, and when?

Caretaking: This item is very important for younger children, especially those age five and under. For infants and toddlers, issues such as diet, nap times, and toilet training need to be addressed. For older preschoolers, other behavioral issues such as peer relationships and bedtimes are important. These issues vary greatly and change rapidly during this time. Parents need to keep each other aware of these changes and their observations. As children get older, the issues may include decisions around TV, telephone, and computer usage or even driving privileges and curfews.

Behavior: This area includes discipline issues in the home, outside of the home, and in school. You can't expect complete uniformity in both homes, but you do need to keep each other informed of your children's behavior. As parents, you can decide together about the general moral and ethical education you want to impart to the children. You may be pleasantly surprised at what values you share about your children's behavior.

Scheduling: Birthday, holiday, and vacation scheduling is one of the biggest problem areas for high-conflict parents to discuss. One bit of general advice is to rarely vary the schedule. If changes must be made, give each other as much notice as possible. Remember that changes in the preplanned schedule should be treated as a request, not a given. If you were going to ask a business partner to change meeting times or other scheduled events, you would politely give plenty of notice and help to work out any inconveniences. High-conflict parents have a hard time adapting to changes without feeling suspicious or using the schedule adjustment as an opportunity to thwart the other parent's plans with the children.

Discipline: Parents may handle behavior differently in their own homes. Differences in culture, background, and view may create two very unique environments. The children may need to get used to these differences and adjust accordingly. Nevertheless, you need to keep each other informed of how you are handling the children's behavior. Believe it or not, you may even be helpful by sharing what works when you are with the children. You might save each other some time and energy. You might also increase the consistency with which the children are treated. Two heads solving problems and imparting knowledge to one another make for the most expedient business approach.

New business: This area is reserved for those items that may come up week to week, or on a periodic basis.

Of course you may be saying, "This is all well and good, but how do we avoid falling into the old traps of conflictual communication that we have grown to know and love so well?" Remember, this call is an opportunity to get some things accomplished, not to vent your emotions. In other words, you need to stay the course and avoid discussing old relationship concerns. No zingers, no sarcasm, and above all, no deviations from the agreed-upon agenda. One useful technique is to keep a pad of paper in front of you during the telephone call. You can write down anything that comes to mind, such as all those horrible names and thoughts that you just may have about the other parent or what they are saying. Then, *don't say it!* The thoughts can't turn the tide of the conversation toward conflict, but the words certainly will. You can write whatever you want, but just refrain from reading it to the other parent. Keeping the conversation on track is obviously in the best interests of your children. It will also lead to shorter calls!

Some parents ask to have this parenting call in writing, by e-mail, or via instant messaging. In the few cases where the conflict level is so high that conversation is not tolerable, this may have to be initially acceptable. It is certainly not preferable and in our experience has had minimal long-term success. However, parents may need to communicate some issues in between phone calls, and at these times faxing, e-mail, voice mail, or writing may be necessary. In general, parents need to work toward having civil conversations about their children. After all, the silent technique in business doesn't get the job done. You would never be able to decide that you are not going to talk to a business colleague with whom you had to work on an important project. Can you imagine how cumbersome it would be if you had to conduct a lifelong assignment only through written communication and never talk or meet in person to discuss important issues and make decisions? The company would be burdened by the complicated process by which it did business, and the employees and the product would suffer from the extreme lack of efficiency.

Remember the old telephone game that you played as a child? In the game, a message is passed along from one person to the next, usually by whispering in the person's ear. By the time the message gets to the last person and is announced out loud, it usually sounds completely different from the original statement. Parents play this game in their communications about children and other issues during and after divorce. If these slight variations are then communicated to attorneys and they begin to act on your behalf, the sparks can fly. Therefore, it may be a good idea to write a summary of your parenting call and exchange that with the other parent. The parent who is in charge of the agenda for that call could be the secretary for that meeting or you could just alternate that responsibility.

Finally, remember to clarify or establish the time and date of the next call so that there are no misperceptions about the schedule. This is especially important in the beginning when these calls are new and awkward and more subject to high-conflict parental tactics.

You may find it helpful to use the form below to both plan your agenda and record your decisions.

Parenting Agenda

Week of:		
Category	**This Week's Issues/Info**	**Decisions**
Good Stuff		
Medical		
School		
Activities		
Caretaking		
Behavior		
Scheduling		
Discipline		
New business		
Next Call (Date/Time):		

The Roles of Attorneys and the Courts

Attorneys certainly mean well and are trying to do their job in the best way possible. Nevertheless, you are the parents, and while you are working together to formulate an improved communication system, the attorneys can contribute to the conflict either directly or indirectly. For example, let's imagine that you make some decisions on your parenting call. You decide to check it out with your attorney, who advises you differently. You then go back to your parenting partner with a revision. The other parent may start to feel that any agreements made on the parenting call can't be trusted. Aside from that, your role as the parents becomes subject to a legal opinion and your own confidence is undermined. Married parents don't call their attorney to make decisions about their children. Please remember that the two of you know your children better than anyone else. Of course, this is not to say that there is never a time to seek legal consultation. When you do call your attorney, be thoughtful, aware, and confident. Your attorney is a legal advisor, not a parenting advisor. Parents need to be responsible for parenting.

The courts are often drawn into being the decision makers on too many issues that belong in the parental domain. It is important not to abdicate your own responsibility as parents to a higher authority just because reaching a compromise solution is arduous. That statement, "I'll see you in court," is said all too easily and without consideration of the potentially adverse consequences. Court decisions aren't always going to be in your favor, so why take that risk? In business you wouldn't immediately throw disputed decisions up to a higher level of management. You wouldn't go to court or arbitration except in very unusual circumstances. If you appealed to the higher-ups at work too many times, the person to whom you report would probably get annoyed and feel that you are taking up too much of his or her time. You might be viewed as being too difficult to work with, or having too little confidence in your own decisions. You might get the reputation of not being a team player, or being just plain lazy. Whatever the case, you'd be smart to get your résumé together, because you'd probably be on the way out. If you come to court with trivial matters, the judge too may get exasperated and take over, offering very little flexibility. You then lose a good part of your job as parents and lose much of your say in the lives of your children. When these children were born you most certainly did not expect them to be raised by the decisions of a judge. While judges will support your attempts to work together as parents in the business of parenting your children, they don't want to do your job.

Lastly, let's address the role of attorneys for the minor children and guardians *ad litem*. Certain decisions are quite difficult and complicated, such as changes in parenting plans. These specialized attorneys can be wonderful consultants, giving excellent advice and expressing the interests and desires of your children. They will work with you and guide you if you make it clear that you want to continue to exercise your role as real parents.

A Dozen Golden Parent Agreement Rules

Most of the literature on co-parenting discusses sets of rules (Blau 1993; Ricci 1980) to follow when interacting with the other parent or when dealing with the children. These rules are designed to provide a structure for your interactions and to prevent conflict. They are crucial, simple fundamentals that need to be adhered to at all times to prevent hurting the children. Their simplicity makes them easy to accept, and few parents ever say that they don't want to follow them. They would find it hard to argue that the rules aren't in their children's best interests. However, the dynamics of high-conflict relationships are such that the rules are easily broken. It is a good idea to keep these rules close at hand so that you can refer to them whenever fighting impulses arise. Melinda Blau's book (1996) provides daily meditations for parents that can keep you focused on the behaviors that will enhance co-parenting relationships. Do whatever is necessary to make sure that the children's needs are treated with the respect that they are due. You wouldn't talk to a colleague or client in ways that would inflame them, nor would you interfere with their work or their relationships with shared personnel. You would work with them and figure out how to get the results you want and need. You need to treat your co-parent the same way.

The following are our recommendations for rules of conduct as co-parents. These rules should be reviewed and formally signed by both parents.

We Will Treat Each Other with Respect at All Times

The key to this parenting rule is cordiality. Parents must interact with each other in ways that demonstrate the fundamentals of acceptable social interaction. This means greeting each other nicely and exchanging pleasantries in front of the children. Both parents need to routinely act in a manner that models appropriate behavior between two adults. Remember that your children will treat you and the other parent in the same way that you treat one another. In addition, you are providing them with an example of how to approach other adults in their lives in school, athletics, work, etc. Common decency is the only acceptable principle to follow when working with or talking with the other parent. Anything less than that can be harmful to your children's welfare and will contribute to a pattern of conflict, which will have a negative emotional impact on their future relationships with you and others in their lives.

We Will Not Use Condescending or Derogatory Terms in Exchanges with Each Other

This too is a very simple rule! Do not speak to each other in inflammatory ways. High-conflict parents often feel free to say insulting, attacking things to one another that they would never say to anyone else in their lives. They use language that is not acceptable in any other areas of their lives. They feel free to call the other parent names, use slang, use four-letter words, and heap criticism upon the other parent. These are just more attempts to spray anger and to control the other parent. Every time that a parent hurls a hurtful remark at the other parent, every time a parent refers to the other parent in a derogatory manner, and every time a parent peppers their exchange with expletives, they need to remember how much they are affecting their children's futures. Keep your children's faces in front of you at all times (pull out their pictures if needed) and STOP before you say things that contribute to a level of conflict that will become harder and harder to repair.

We Agree to Make Our Children's Needs More Important Than Our Own Territorial Needs or Needs for Independence

Your children's lives continue during and beyond your divorce. Your lives as parents should therefore continue to be dictated (to a reasonable degree) by the children's needs and schedules. Their lives should go on in as routine a way as possible. Their activities, school requirements, and peer relationships are still important to them and their development. You have to adapt to meet their needs and to participate in their lives, a concept that is hard for parents who insist on thinking about their parenting schedule as *"my* time with the children." They see every party, practice, activity, and school function as an imposition. They believe that the other parent is trying to take away their time with the children, make their life complicated, and interfere with their parenting relationship. Some parents are just not used to adapting their world to work well for the children, even if that means that they may have to miss a business meeting or a social engagement. Many parents try to balance their new lives, a quest for privacy, and their need for new relationships with work, the parenting schedule, and the demands of family and friends. Children can become pawns in this process and are often used as objects through which one parent can get back at the other. Every request for a schedule change, or for help in transportation, or even for the child's participation in a new area of interest, can become a struggle and an opportunity to get back at the other parent. High-conflict parents are often heard saying, "Do not schedule the children for activities on *my* time" or "If Susie goes there, then I will be missing two hours of *my* time." This then provides justification for saying "No" to the other parent and ultimately to the child. Be sure that your decisions are truly based on your vision of the well-being of your children and your knowledge of them. Decisions should not be made out of your desire to seize control, to make life difficult for the other parent, or to hurt them with an unnecessary power play. You only hurt the children and your relationship with them.

We Agree to Respect the Other Parent's Time with Our Children and Not Interfere with the Scheduled Agreement

High-conflict parents and their children need their parenting schedule—it provides glue and structure, and it helps keep the conflict in check. Aside from this, parents have lives too. They need a plan around which they can go forward with work, their social life, and new relationships. Keeping to the schedule also helps to build trust by reinforcing both parents' commitment to the process and their respect for each other. Nevertheless, the most important reason to keep to the schedule is the consistency it provides the children. They expect you to be there for them and may not have developed the capacity for adapting to schedule changes. This is especially true for toddlers and preschoolers. In addition, schedule changes often are inconvenient and can make life difficult for the other parent. Keep them to a minimum. At times, adjustments are necessary, but the schedule should never be considered as an outline or proposal. It is an agreement. You wouldn't keep changing the schedule on your business partner. As in business, reliability and constancy make for success in co-parenting.

We Agree to Respect the Other Parent's Parenting Style and Discuss Any Concerns at Agreed-Upon Communication Times

On the one hand, you as parents may strive for consistency in raising the children in two different homes, but you also have to realize that this goal is somewhat elusive. High-conflict parents often have a serious degree of difference in parenting style. They blame, criticize, and accuse each other of not caring for the children properly, corrupting the children, or not providing a safe environment for the children. Many times this is just a reflection of two diametrically opposed parenting approaches. Remember, you divorced (or were never married) for a reason. Sometimes you just have to agree to differ on particular points, to allow you to focus on bringing about a greater level of uniformity in other areas. Relatively easy areas to agree on are daily care, scheduling, and homework. The harder areas to agree on are discipline and peer relationships. Children learn to adapt to these differences and may even learn a valuable lesson by being exposed to different viewpoints. Or they may use these differences to manipulate you both as co-parents. Be aware of what's going on in the other home but don't try to parent the children over each other's doorstep. No one has cornered the market on parenting, and believe it or not, you *can* learn from each other. Sometimes a method that works in one household can replace a tired and ineffective practice used by the other parent. Save your questions for your parenting call and *never* make evaluative statements about the other parent's approach in front of the children.

Any Disagreements or Areas of Potential Conflict Will Only Be Discussed at Designated Times and Not in Front of or in Earshot of the Children

This is a rule that we discussed in much detail earlier. *Never* expose the children to your conflicts. High-conflict parents engage in hostile interactions, not the usual form of healthy disagreement. They rarely demonstrate the capacity to have a simple discussion in front of the children. Your conflicts upset the children and put them in an untenable situation, so save your feelings for protected times when the children are not privy to your tension. Remember, they need to heal from the effects of the divorce and the marital struggles, and they need a chance to recover without being constantly reminded of your continued animosity. Act like adults and protect your children. Without this protection they may experience anxiety and depressive symptoms, which may require professional intervention.

We Agree to Follow the Parenting Schedule by Always Being on Time for the Children

This rule seemed so crucial that we gave it a place of its own. Your life is important, but remember, so are those of the other parent and the children. It is not appropriate to be more than fifteen minutes late in most other areas of your life, so have the same level of respect for your co-parent and the children. Give each other reasonable lee-way, but make every effort to be there when you say you will. In fact, we often recommend that high-conflict parents be five minutes early. Your children are counting on you to pick them up or drop them off. They should never be "left on the doorstep." The other parent may need to leave for work, a meeting, or some other activity, and you need to be there at the agreed upon times and places. Again, teach your children the importance of timeliness and dependability by your own actions.

Any Changes to the Schedule Must Be Discussed with the Other Parent First, Prior to Informing the Children

When high-conflict parents are having difficulty communicating, they often rely on the children to convey information to the other parent. Parents are then placing the children in the role that should really be reserved for the other parent. They tend to discuss schedule changes and other issues directly with the children before they check it out with the other parent. Of course, the children are therefore privy to knowing the possible plans first and may be disappointed if the changes are not made. They can blame the parent who cannot or is not willing to accommodate the change. On the other hand, if the change is not something that the child wants, he/she has a chance to react before the other parent even has a chance at bat. Scheduling issues, vacations, and changes to the parenting plan must be discussed by the parents first. The decisions should be formalized before you present the information to the children. Older children (ages ten and over) may be involved in some discussions to give input where the parents deem appropriate. Remember that the child's opinion is just input and not the final word. You, as *parents*, get that privilege—like it or not!

We Agree Never to Say Negative Things about the Other Parent to or in Front of the Children

This is probably one of the most important parental rules. Children do not appreciate it if you insist on degrading the other parent by making unkind and critical remarks. They need and want to believe that both of their parents are doing the best that they can do to parent them. During a divorce, children are often less confident in their own judgment and also in their parents' ability to care for them successfully. When you undermine the other parent, you take away the little confidence the child has and instead you ask them to join in a vendetta against the other parent. This and other behaviors can form the beginnings of what is called parent alienation syndrome. In high-conflict parent situations, parents break this rule constantly by taking most any opportunity to demean the other parent. This ranges from making snide personal remarks to citing specific behaviors of the other parent to which they object.

An example of this was recognized by Ann Landers in her response to a letter (published in the *Hartford Courant*, February 23, 2000). A "Dad in Ohio" wrote that his ex-wife was a liar as well as "conniving and manipulative." He reported that he told the children, "Your mother loves you very much, but she has a problem telling the truth. . . ." He went on to say that his approach of educating the children about their mother's shortcomings had been successful, ending his letter by saying, "Believe me, it works." Ann Landers wisely responded by discouraging the father's actions. She stated, "Children of divorce have a tough enough time without having a father who berates ... their mother. So, please hold the cheap shots, Dad. Those kids have enough to deal with."

Our Child/Children Will Not Be Placed in Any Loyalty Conflicts and Will Not Be Encouraged Overtly or Subtly to Take One Parent's Side Against the Other

Your children are not pawns in a high-stakes chess game. Children of high-conflict parents are frequently victims of loyalty conflicts. They are caught up in the process of trying to say or do what they think will please one parent vs. the other. They go back and forth between both homes communicating information, comments, and offhand remarks—whatever they believe will win that parent's support. This only puts the children in a position where they cannot be believed by anyone. Yet, high-conflict parents want to believe their children and often do. They quote the children, believing the comments to be true, and then they leap into the conflict arena. The children must *not* be the conveyors of parental information. Do not ask them what goes on in the other home in order to secure information. Rather than immediately believing that what they say is true, check it out with the other parent first. Children who are placed in loyalty conflicts are more prone to emotional difficulties. They can't even rely on themselves to know or tell the truth. Their parents may reinforce this manipulative behavior for their own interests and satisfaction.

Are you willing to sacrifice your children to support leftover anger at the other parent?

It Is in Our Child/Children's Best Interests to Have Two Parents Who Love and Care for Them Involved in Their Lives on a Regular Basis

Co-parenting always presupposes this rule. Postdivorce, this is your child's best shot at a successful resolution. Unless one of you is clearly unfit, surgical removal of a parent is not in the best interests of your child. Co-parenting is even more complicated than parenting in general. The lives of your children are complicated logistically and emotionally. They need you both and *you* need you both. Together, you can preserve the children's need to feel secure and loved by both parents and not force them to choose between you. This is what you expected for them when they were born, and this is what they deserve—even though you are no longer married.

We Understand That We May Be Divorced, Separated, or Never Married, but We Will Always Be the Parents Together for the Duration of our Lives or the Lives of the Children

You created these children together and you will be their parents together for the duration. The end of the marriage did not end your parenting relationship together. In high-conflict cases, it may feel preferable at times to parent singly. You may believe you can make your own decisions, lead your own life, not answer to anyone else, and seek no other consultation. You feel you are on your own with the children. When the hostility level gets high, this starts to sound awfully good. Nevertheless, you cannot make this choice unilaterally. The other parent is your parenting business partner, like it or not. Develop a good working relationship and get the business of parenting done well. Throughout the children's lives there will be times when you must come together: recitals, graduation, illnesses, marriages, grandchildren, etc. Be sure you are there together for all of the events and issues in their lives. As the adults in this situation, you must approach each other with the same business acumen that you would when working with your most challenging colleague.

The above parenting rules are *not* optional. They are necessities. High-conflict parents have great difficulty following these rules and often try to bend them to meet their own needs, because they expect flexibility from others but have problems being flexible themselves. They truly possess creative genius when it comes to rule interpretation. In one case cited by an attorney, the parents were told by the attorney for the minor children not to pass messages to each other through the older son. They agreed. The next week they didn't send messages to each other through their oldest son, but instead sent them through the middle son! In a high-conflict parenting situation, you shouldn't take anything for granted. You must make sure that the definitions, even basic "common sense" definitions, are clearly understood by both of you. Many high-conflict parents say that they agree with the above rules and are ready to sign on the dotted line, but in truth they are only giving lip service to the issues. After all, how can they express disagreement with these rules? They are straightforward and clearly in the best interests of the children. Yet overt agreement coupled with covert disagreement can be disastrous.

These rules can help you achieve collaboration and allow you to effectively master the business of co-parenting after divorce. Remember that it is easy to focus on the other parent's behavior and forget to evaluate your own honestly. Be careful and self-critical. Do not always blame the upset or misunderstanding on the other guy. You are in control of your own choices, words, and actions. Seize that control and use it wisely.

Part II

Co-Parenting
Guidelines

CHAPTER 6

Making Parenting Plans Work

What Is a Parenting Plan?

They are also known as "visitation plans" or "custody arrangements." They are the building blocks of the structure for spending time with and caring for the children. These plans are often provisionally established during separation, finalized at the divorce, and then modified after the divorce.

Parenting plans are a point in the divorce where conflict breeds as if it were a virus or infection. Try telling a parent, "You can't see your children when you want to." Or, "Someone you don't trust or like is going to be taking care of your children when you are not." Quite naturally, there is a lot of negative emotion linked to the parenting plan.

High-conflict parents often spend considerable energy arguing over and negotiating parenting plans. If they cannot reach an equitable solution, outside professionals are called in to make recommendations. These recommendations often follow a custody evaluation that can easily cost upwards of $7,000 and take months to complete. Some parents have had more than one custody evaluation in order to have someone else tell them how and when they each should spend time with the children. Additionally, other basic details are often determined by the court. For example, the court or family relations officers might set the time of day and the place where the transitions should occur. Rules are spelled out concerning school vacations, holiday schedules, birthdays, etc. In fact, most of the details surrounding how and when the children will be with each parent are determined in advance. You probably have a similar document that outlines your arrangement.

Why Is It So Difficult?

Things Change

Unfortunately, parenting plan documents quickly become outdated. The children's schedules and needs change. As the children get older, they have different developmental needs. They need different levels of supervision, struggle with ever-increasing levels of independence, and change how they interact with their parents. Parents have other obligations that necessitate a change in the plan. Job and career issues may come into play and interfere with previously made schedules. There may be opportunities for relocation. One or both parents may remarry and have a need to change the schedule. Special events may also lead one or both parents to seek to modify the plan.

We're Emotional

Can any of us be truly objective when it comes to our children? We are biased in the best of circumstances, but when we add the stress of conflict, objectivity can be almost impossible. Communication between parents often seems like a golden opportunity to get back at each other. You might find that after the divorce you have the same arguments with the other parent and feel the same way that you did when you were married. You may be accidentally rehashing the same old issues in your communications with each other. The same emotions come to the surface and dominate your interactions with each other. Parents often continue to try to "make it right" or get after the divorce what they could not get in the marriage.

It Must Be Fair

There is an illusion for many parents and divorce professionals that the amount of time each parent spends with the children should be equal. This does not occur in intact families. Often one parent spends much more time with the children than the other, so why should it be equal in a divorce? The concept of equal time causes many problems. Parents start counting the days and even hours they are with, or not with, the children. They look at available "quality" time and they look at vacation and holiday times. They add in or subtract out carpooling time, activity time, etc., to suit the argument they are trying to make. "You took the child to [activity] on my day, so I should get equal time on one of your days."

"When You Have the Kids, I'm Missing Something"

What do you miss when the children are not with you? First steps, a smile, an opportunity to dry a tear, a good-night kiss, a joke, a hug, witnessing one of ten thousand accomplishments, a chance to get closer to parts of your children's lives that are not available to you when your children are not with you. You may feel incredibly sad when you think about these parts of your children's lives. In divorce, everyone misses something. Both parents miss large pieces of their children's lives. The children miss pieces of their parents' lives. Low-conflict parents offset this by communicating well with each other. High-conflict parents communicate poorly and miss more and more. Your children miss more as well. They miss the chance to see the smile on both parents' faces after an accomplishment. They miss getting two hugs. Sometimes they miss getting two lectures, even if they don't want either of them.

It's Visitation Time, Not Parenting Time

"You know you have to go. It's in the court order. You have to spend time with your [other parent]. It's called visitation. I've packed your suitcase. Come on, [other parent] will be here in a few minutes," says the parent to the child.

We have called the time with one parent "visitation" for so long that we begin to believe that it is a "visit." It has become something optional, and at times it's a nuisance. "Why go through the pain or the hassle? It's just not worth it."

The concept of "visitation" devalues the relationship of both parents with the children. This devaluing can further contribute to the conflict as the parents fight for "their time" with the children instead of supporting the other parent's role in their children's lives. Truly, the time with each parent is *parenting time*. Parents may have different styles and may use the time differently (just like in intact families) but they continue in the role of parents. Your children are not "visitors" in your home or in their other parent's home. They live there! They belong with both of you. High-conflict parents often give the power of parenting away. The concept of a "visit" leaves one or both parents feeling as if they do not really have influence over their own children. It can leave the children feeling as if they are constantly on the move. They can begin to resent both of you for putting them in this position.

Holidays Are Special Challenges

We give special meaning to holidays. These are family times when we spend extra-special moments with each other. They are times when we remind each other to be grateful. They are times when we remember how life has changed. There may be new babies at the dinner table, and grandparents may no longer be with us. These days often have a history as they are traditional times to be together with extended family and friends. The special symbolism, traditions, and expectations bring an emotionality to the holiday.

Yet after a divorce, these times are particularly stressful. Reminders of the changes that have occurred abound. To be without one's children is exceptionally stressful and painful. It is a grim reminder of how life has changed. Even being without one's spouse can be stressful when everyone else is paired. The children are stressed as well, because they see the changes. Even if the children are with you, the holiday can be a reminder of the divorce as you and they look around the dinner table and see other intact families there together.

Extended family members may make comments, look at you with pity or scorn, or act in a way that is insensitive. You may feel the pressure and possible embarrassment of having to say, "The kids? Oh, they are with [other parent] today."

Parents will often fight over the holidays. "The children need to be with me." You might say or hear, "This holiday is special. It is an exception. Would you deprive [child] of this special opportunity, just because it is your day?" Conflict-addicted parents will often find that holidays can be a recurring opportunity to take advantage of or retaliate against each other. The holidays become another vehicle for victimizing or being victimized.

Special Problems of High-Conflict Parents

Counting Hours

Tallying the hours each parent is with the child is one of the practices that contributes to conflict addiction. It implies that everything has to be exactly fair. It implies that exactly 50/50 time with each parent is always best for the children. It implies that "*My* time with the children is more important than what the children may be doing in *their* lives." Counting the hours also makes you focus on the quantity of time you and the other parent are with the children, rather than what is best for the children.

In a divorce, the assets of the family are divided. Unfortunately, the children cannot be divided. So instead we divide the time each parent has with the children. At the time of the divorce, all the other assets are divided with some degree of permanence. You get the sofa and I get the TV and VCR. After the divorce there is little dispute or need to change the division of these assets. Yet, when it comes to parenting time, the arguments over the division of this asset become continual for high-conflict parents. Each fifteen minutes becomes another battle as if it were detrimental to the child to use that time with one parent or the other.

Imagine going to a business dinner. You order the steak and I order the seafood. You have a regular salad and I have a Caesar salad. You have a glass of wine and I have water. I have dessert and you have coffee. Including tax and tip the total bill is $47.89. Your meal is $26.32. My meal is $21.57. What does it communicate if we split the bill based on the exact cost of each of our meals? What does it communicate if we split the bill exactly 50/50? What does it communicate if we just split the bill in a way that is most convenient? Which way promotes a better business relationship? Should it be fair to the penny (or minute)? Or, in the spirit of a positive working relationship, should we share the bill in a way that makes sense? Sometimes, it is best if we don't even split the bill. Maybe one of us should just pay for this meal in its entirety. Perhaps counting the hours is getting in the way of clearly seeing your children's needs.

Leaving Your Child with Someone You Don't Trust

There is almost no other situation in which a parent would leave their child for extended periods of time with someone they do not trust. Baby-sitters, daycare centers, and nannies are interviewed and often observed before a child is left in their care. Yet, high-conflict parents are, by necessity, forced to leave their children with people they do not trust. This causes doubt and suspicion. There can be implications that one of you is not taking care of the children in a responsible fashion. You may hear or say:

"What do you mean, they didn't have a bath?"

"They didn't have dinner?"

"How did you punish them?"

"Why didn't they get to play with their friends?"

"You put them to bed at what time?"

"I understand you didn't help them with their homework."

"You fed them what?"

These statements—and the doubt and suspicion that surround them—are often a result of poor communication between parents. The children may be communicating some distorted information to the parents. The parents may communicate incompletely and irregularly. They are likely to fill in the blanks with negative impressions and thoughts.

"My Children Should Be with Me!"

As long as you hold on to the belief that your children are better off with you, it will be difficult to rationalize or comprehend why they should be with their other parent. You will probably fight this every step of the way. Each visit becomes a lost battle in the war of divorce. Each visit may also become a chance that your children will discover that, "It really isn't half bad at [other parent]'s. I actually had more fun there." Each visit therefore becomes threatening to you. It is a chance that you will, in some way, lose your children to the other parent. There is considerable conscious and unconscious motivation to keep visitation with the other parent to a minimum.

Problems Exchanging Information

"I was waiting for you for forty-five minutes. Where were you? Why didn't you call and tell me you were going to be late?"

"I told you last week I needed the children two hours earlier today. Now you tell me I can't have them?"

"What do you mean the soccer tournament is today? I had plans to take the children to see Aunt Marie."

"You didn't tell me [child] had a paper due for school. We didn't do it."

Do any of these sound familiar? Parenting plans often become problematic when information is not effectively exchanged. There are more opportunities for one parent to feel slighted or victimized. It creates distrust and resentment (feelings that are already in abundance). Parents then position themselves against each other. They don't take responsibility for seeing that important information is exchanged. They create more problems and more confusion.

Control Issues

"If you think I'm going to give in on this one, you've got another thing coming!"

"I know you're just trying to take advantage. Forget it. No way!"

Parents have different styles of dealing with conflict. You may quickly dig your heels in when you feel threatened. At times, this can cause you to make decisions subjectively, and ostensibly for the "principle" of it, rather than in the best interests of the children. Decisions made this way are not necessarily effective.

Other parents are in quiet conflict. These parents do not yell or scream. They do not speak in a particularly hostile fashion to each other. Instead, they rarely give in or give just an inch. They may say, "We have a plan. Let's stick to it." They use the parenting plan to enforce rigidity and to take control. These parents often avoid making new decisions to solve problems.

Regardless of your conflict style, the control battle becomes a continuation of the divorce. It becomes another chance to win. Unfortunately, it also becomes another chance to avoid making a decision. Do you argue over what time the children should be brought to the other parent's home? Can one of you make it at 5:30 P.M. but the other can only make it at 6:00 P.M.? Even 5:45 P.M. will not work. High-conflict parents need to put aside the control battle. Would you stick to this position with an important client or customer? Would you hold fast on an important project at work? If your best friend from high school were flying into town, wouldn't you rearrange your schedule? Is it really true that you cannot be flexible? Or is it more like, "I'm not going to give in again"?

Difficulties in Solving Day-to-Day Problems

High-conflict parents often say, "I'd rather just take care of it myself." The conflict can be draining. The failed attempts to negotiate or be reasonable can often leave you feeling as if it is just not worth it. You might find yourself saying, "If the children were just with me, it would be so much easier. I'd take care of what needs to be done. I wouldn't have to try to deal with their [other parent], who is just impossible." The tedium of doing the day-to-day business with the other parent can, at times, seem unbearable. Talking on the phone to coordinate where the athletic equipment should be can be a daunting task. All of these conflictual situations can make you feel drained and distracted—just like when you were married.

In short, high-conflict parents and their children have it worse than other divorced families. Even the basic structure around parenting time and implementing the parenting agreement can be fraught with difficulties. You can turn scheduling, coordinating clothes and equipment, the children's personal schedules, and almost anything else into conflict, or you can choose to neutralize and solve the problems. Remember, if you have the power to engage in conflict, you have the power to *not* engage and to instead solve the problems.

Solving the Problems

Build Trust

Trust develops between high-conflict parents when there is a combination of reliability and reasonable action.

Reliability + Reasonable Action = Trust

Reliability means that the other parent can count on you to do what you say you are going to do. When you behave reliably, you show up on time, convey the information you said you would convey, avoid misleading the other parent, and bring the clothes or other items needed. Reliability is based on the repetition of experience over time. The more you follow through, the more reliability is increased. The one problem with reliability is that one reliable action has much less weight than one unreliable action. If you are on time ten times but late once, the late time will go a long way toward undoing the times you arrived promptly. Would you use a bank that made a mistake on one of ten transactions? Would you use the same take-out restaurant if one out of ten meals were not prepared well? *Consistency* is the key here. You are in control of your own behavior, so make plans you can keep.

Reasonable action is an extremely difficult practice for high-conflict parents. The whole divorce and most elements associated with it may seem unreasonable. The parenting plan does not seem fair to you. The other parent does not act reasonably. Why should you?

First, children need reasonable parents. Decreasing the conflict and building trust around the parenting plan has to start somewhere. If you each wait for the other to start, it will never happen. You will be a victim of the behavior and inaction of the other parent. If your actions are reasonable, there is less chance that you will have difficulty explaining them, have to apologize, or feel guilty. You may make a choice with regard to the children or the parenting plan that does not work out. However, if you behave in a reasonable fashion, it is more likely the choice will be understood. Reasonable action can refer to your actions and the decisions you make with your children, as well as the way you conduct yourself with your children's other parent. Your behavior needs to reflect your values. Your reasonable actions can beget reasonable actions in response.

You need to recognize that the other parent will take care of the children as they see fit. This would be true if you were married. If you were away visiting a relative, there might be dishes in the sink and missed baths. Homework might not get done. Some rules might be ignored. The children would essentially be safe, even if they weren't cared for according to your standards. To build trust, you need to start curtailing any tendency to question and criticize the other parent's actions (or lack thereof). The more you criticize, the more they will defend or fight back. Build trust by recognizing that fighting over what you cannot change is futile.

Trust is not just what you feel; it's what you do. It is about your attitude and the risks you are willing to take. Except in extreme situations, you do not have a choice about whether the children are going to be with their other parent. Your choice is how you are going to solve the problems. Building trust is a first step.

Pay Attention to Child Development

Parenting plans need to be responsive to the developmental needs of your children. Modifications need to take into account the different ways that children respond to stress, change in their lives, and even their parents. Your plan also needs to be sensitive to the effects of transitions. It needs to balance the need for flexibility with the need for the children to have a sense of stability in their lives.

The authors have seen (but would not recommend) plans for four-year-olds where one day they are with one parent and the next day they are with the other parent. This type of plan can leave the child feeling very confused and disoriented. While it may be "fair" to the parents for each of them to see the child for the same number of hours per week, one has to ask whether it's truly best for a four-year-old (or perhaps any age) child.

Similarly, we have seen parents try to rigidly hold on to a plan that may have been appropriate for a twelve-year-old, but is no longer appropriate for their child now that he is sixteen and has a driver's license. As the child matures, more flexibility is usually required. You cannot expect that a parenting plan will work successfully throughout a child's development. Many times we ask a parent to think about whether they would have the same expectation for parenting time if the family were intact. You probably would not expect your teenager to spend one night a week and every other weekend one-on-one with you if you never got divorced. They would have other interests and activities and would not necessarily seek you out on the weekend. They would want to visit with friends instead of spending the weekend just with their parents.

High-conflict parents need to be especially sensitive to the needs of their children. As the children age, their needs for time with each of you may change. When the other parent makes a suggestion, it is important to view it in the context of your child's needs. The other parent is not necessarily trying to "poison" the child against you or trying to take advantage. If you adopt a defensive posture, you will likely miss the opportunity to address your children's actual needs.

Plan for the Holidays

Holidays can be times to begin new traditions and put the conflict aside. Parents can show children that it is possible to rise above the conflict to still make the holidays special. If you agree long before the holidays on how to structure the time, you can concentrate on enjoying the time and making it meaningful, rather than fighting over who has the children when. In our experience, it is best to plan holidays well in advance. The parenting plan should specify a plan for each holiday year by year so the decisions do not have to be renegotiated each year. It is generally better to make one decision one time rather than many decisions many times.

High-conflict parents generally will do better if they keep to a predetermined plan that even specifies the time of day holiday transitions are to occur. Flexibility is a concept that is very difficult to achieve when there is high conflict. Flexibility in the face of the emotionality and sentimentality around a holiday is even more difficult. If a plan is in place, it is best to try to stick to it. If it needs to be changed, we recommend changing it well in advance of the holidays (three to six months in advance) and only if you can mutually agree to the changes. Of course there will be exceptions. There can be a certain holiday event in one household that may be particularly special *this* year. Ideally, you should consider deviating from your plan when a major exception arises.

Respect Differences in Parenting Skills

Parents often have different levels of information and skills. Some were less involved in the day-to-day running of a household when they were married. They may have participated with their children in some after-school activities and may have "helped" with some household chores, but they may not have taken primary responsibility for many aspects of running the household. Divorce puts each parent in the position of having to know all of the information that was typically shared by two people.

A great number of parents refuse to ask for help. They don't ask the people who know best how to provide for their children's daily needs for directions about taking care of the people they love the most. They say, "You've got to be kidding if you think I'm going to ask that *@#!^% for advice."

After divorce, many parents are quite willing to say to their exes, "If you think it's so easy, then go ahead and try." They sit back and let their children suffer as the other parent struggles to balance the complexity of demands associated with the children's lives. They let that parent's learning curve develop at its own pace without giving each other the benefit of their experience. Many times parents have a certain sadistic sense of satisfaction watching each other struggle. This struggle only hurts the children, and doesn't build a sense of teamwork with the other parent.

Instead, consider aiding one another with your individual knowledge. Helping each other can only be helpful to your children. It builds an attitude of teamwork around your most precious assets—your children. Providing useful information and suggestions to each other helps give your children a more stable and enriched life that addresses their needs.

Be Flexible

Life does not fit parenting plans. The most flexible plan cannot accommodate the unforeseen opportunities, trauma, and challenges that life dishes out. Consequently, parents need to recognize that there will be occasions where the plan will not fit the needs of the children. Situations will arise that do not warrant a rewriting of the plan but do warrant consideration of different alternatives. Flexibility is a blessing and curse.

Flexibility allows parents to adjust the plan to fit the needs of the children and the demands of the moment. Sometimes this relates specifically to circumstances that affect the children. Other times it relates to situations in your life. For example, this afternoon your boss asks you to stay late and work on a major project. But you are supposed to pick up the children at 5 P.M. and return them to their other parent at 9 P.M. What do you do? You can say "no" to the boss and miss a major business opportunity. You can call a baby-sitter to pick up the children and give them dinner. Instead, imagine calling the one person in the world who has as much investment in your children as you do: their other parent. What if you called and asked if they could take care of the children tonight? Could you exchange tonight for another night? What if you couldn't make an "even" exchange? Might it still be better to have the children stay with their other parent? Might it be a sign of good will? Might it help you build your working relationship with their other parent?

The curse of flexibility is that it requires you to work together. It requires joint decision making and joint problem solving. It can contribute to conflict if you and the other parent use this as an opportunity to keep score and find fault with one another. If you keep score, then the request for flexibility also becomes a transaction that goes on the tally sheet. "How many breaks did I give you? How many did you give me? Who owes the other now?" The decision is then based on the tally and the perceived advantage, not on what is best for the children. The request becomes one more opportunity for conflict. It becomes one more opportunity to "pay back" the other parent. It is one more opportunity for revenge.

The following is an example of two different styles of communicating about vacation times. See which example fits your typical interaction with your children's other parent. Pay attention to the different choices each parent makes in their use of language and tone with each other.

The situation: Mother is, according to the parenting plan, entitled this year to pick her two weeks of summer vacation, before father. However, she is able to get a third week of vacation off from her employer and would like to take a third week. If she takes a third week father will miss his usual days with the children. Mother also wants to use this third week to take two weeks in a row.

Example 1

Mother:	So, I've decided which weeks I want for summer vacation.
Father:	Yeah?
Mother:	I want the week of July 10 and the week of August 15.
Father:	Okay.
Mother:	Well, there's something else.
Father:	I figured.
Mother:	I'm able to get the week of August 22 off too. I'd like to take the kids for that week too.

Father:	(Smiling) I don't think so. Why should I not see them for three weeks? You've got two weeks coming to you. That's what you get.
Mother:	But I can get the time. What should I do, just sit home?
Father:	That's okay with me. I couldn't care less. Do whatever you want. It's not my problem.
Mother:	So you're telling me you'd rather the kids do nothing that week, rather than have an extra week of vacation?
Father:	There you go, putting words in my mouth. I'm not saying that at all. The agreement says you pick your two weeks and then I pick mine. It doesn't say anything about three weeks. Plus, what week did you say you wanted for the third week?
Mother:	The week of August 22.
Father:	Well, that was one of the weeks I was thinking of taking anyway.
Mother:	Yeah, right! All you want to do is get back at me. You don't care who you hurt or how it affects the kids. You're an #*!$%. You'll never change!
Father:	Well, you're a %^&*@. The agreement says two weeks each. Two weeks it is. You can just forget it!

The same parents could choose to have the interaction play out differently.

Example 2

Mother:	I'd like to discuss summer vacation. I have some ideas about doing something differently than the agreement and in a way where maybe we both could have more vacation time with the kids. I'm hoping we can come to an agreement.
Father:	What do you have in mind?
Mother:	Well, the agreement says that we each get two weeks of vacation with the kids. This year it is my turn to pick the weeks first. I would like the week

of July 10 and the week of August 15. But I've got an opportunity that I'd like to talk about.

Father: What's that?

Mother: Well, my boss said I could also take a third week off if I wanted to during the summer. The week of August 22 would be fine with work. I was thinking that if we could work it out maybe the kids could be with each of us for three weeks instead of two. They'd get more vacation time and we'd see them for more time.

Father: What if I can't get three weeks off?

Mother: Well, I thought about that too. If you can't get three weeks off, maybe we could trade days so you could see them more days on other weeks over the summer so it would all work out the same.

Father: You mean, I'd get extra days on other weeks.

Mother: Yes. That way it would all work out the same and the kids would have more vacation.

Father: Well, why don't we say you've got the weeks of July 10 and August 15 for now. The idea sounds good to me, but let me check with work to see if I can get one of the first weeks in August as one of my weeks. I wanted to take them some time in August, and the week of August 29 is right at the end, just before school starts, so that week wouldn't work.

Mother: Sounds good. If you can't get at least one of them let me know. Maybe I could switch the week of August 22 for the week of July 17.

Father: I'll check with work tomorrow and let you know so we can get this finalized right away.

Mother: Great.

Father: It looks like we'll be able to give the kids a great summer.

Is the second example impossible? It may seem so, but it's not. It is based on parents concentrating on solving problems and being considerate of one another and the children. It is not based on trust, liking each other, or not feeling betrayed in the past. The parents in Example 2 simply stayed focused on the matters at hand. They looked to have a win/win outcome. Rather than fight, they proposed solutions that were reasonable. They were each willing to be flexible.

Below are some guidelines for creating flexibility and negotiating changes in the parenting plan. You may find it useful to create your proposals by using these guidelines as a template. You can actually write out what you want to say so that you are clear before you begin to present it to your children's other parent.

Guidelines for Flexibility: Proposing Changes

- Give notice that you would like to discuss a change. Remember, you are asking for a favor. You are not in the position to make a demand.

- Restate what is already in place. You should begin with a common understanding of the current situation.

- Be clear and realistic about how this change is beneficial for the children.

- Before stating what you would like, consider the other person's interests. What would your objections be if the other parent were making this request? What consideration would you want to see if you were going to let them do what you want to do?

- State your request clearly and without sarcasm or insults. Keep the change clear and simple and immediately offer the consideration to the other parent.

- Be willing to be flexible yourself. You should have a "Plan B." It is possible the other parent will offer a variation on what you suggest. Actually, their variation could be better than what you have suggested. Remember that the two of you together might come up with something that is better than either one of you would think of on your own.

- Do not wait until the last minute.

- Give the other parent time to see if the change can reasonably be implemented. Don't demand an answer right away.

- Confirm that the two of you have the same understanding of the change. Do not just assume you understand each other.

- Thank the other parent for considering the change (that's right, even if it doesn't work out).

Elements of Successful Parenting Plans

We have found that the best parenting plans have some common elements. If these elements are considered in the initial plan or in the modifications, there seems to be a much better chance that the plan can be routinely and effectively implemented.

Clear and Simple

Can you describe your plan to a second-grader in terms they can understand so they can correctly repeat it back to you? You may say, "I don't have a second-grader." That may be so, but when you are stressed and when there is disagreement and conflict, the plan needs to be simple and clear. Elements of the plan should not be left open to interpretation. Transitions should be done the same way each day. Does your plan sound like the plan below?

> **Plan A:** Father will see the children on alternate weekends beginning Friday at 5 P.M. On those weekends he will return the children to mother at 8 P.M. on Sunday evening. The children will be with him overnight on Tuesdays. They will reside with mother on all other days except on Thursdays of the week in which they will not be with father on the subsequent weekend. On those Thursdays, father will pick them up after school. Mother will pick them up at [the local supermarket] at 8:30 P.M.

The above plan is not a complete parenting plan. It only addresses routine parenting time. What are the potential problems with this plan?

- It does not specify how the children will get to father on Fridays.

- It does not specify how the children will be returned to mother on Sunday.

- The children are returned to mother's on Sunday evening and alternate Thursdays essentially just to sleep. What might be perceived as "two extra nights that they are with their mom" are not times that they truly have access to her. They are bathing, getting ready for bed, and then getting ready for school. Is that worth the time and energy of a transition? They might be better off staying at father's and going to school on the following day from his house.

- It implies they will "visit" with father.

- It does not specify how and when the children will get to father on Tuesdays. Do they have to bring their clothes to school?

- It does not specify where and when the children will be picked up on Thursdays. Is it after school at the school? Is it at home after they take the bus home?

- It has the transitions occur in different places.

- The parents need to meet to make the transitions.

- It has everyone keep track of which weeks the "Thursday exception" takes place.

In short, this plan is not simple or clear. It has too many places where confusion can occur. If your plan sounds like the plan above, consider what modifications can make it more clear. The same plan could be rewritten as follows:

Plan B: The children will spend alternate weekends with each parent beginning immediately after school on Friday. They will go to school on Monday morning from that parent's home. They will go to father's from school on Tuesdays and spend the night at his home. On weeks where they will be spending the weekend with mother, they will also stay at father's the preceding Wednesday night and go to school on Thursday morning from his home. Each parent will provide clothes and other belongings so that the children do not have to transport their things from one parent's home to the other. Each parent will be responsible to see to it that the children are transported safely to or from school when the children are going to school or coming home from school to that parent's home.

Plan B can work better for high-conflict parents. It does not require as many face-to-face meetings. Some avoidance can limit the chance for negative comments. Having fewer transitions also limits the chances that a parent will be late and cause additional resentment. By having belongings at both homes, parents do not have to argue about clothes that are not returned or clothes that are not sent.

Feasible

The plan needs to be designed such that each parent can meet its requirement. A plan shouldn't require parents to show up at 5 P.M. unless this is reasonable for both parents. Can both parents leave their jobs in time to meet by 5 P.M.? Given the situational demands placed on one or both parents, does the time need to be later? If father works second shift, or works late on Wednesday nights, is it reasonable to expect him to be able to care for the children on Wednesdays, or should the plan be different? The plan needs to be written in a way that works.

A plan that is not feasible for *both* of you is not feasible at all. Parents need to make sure the plan makes sense to both of them from a practical standpoint. If you realistically and routinely cannot make a specific pickup time, make the time later. It is better to choose a time that is fifteen minutes later and be five minutes early than a set time fifteen minutes earlier and be ten minutes late. High-conflict parents often unintentionally create conflict by setting up unrealistic parenting plans.

Addresses the Needs of the Children

Many parents and their attorneys fight for plans that address the needs of the parents. They say, "I need to see my children more. It should be 50/50. I don't care what my ex wants, I need what I need." This attitude ignores what the children need. If, for example, the after-school activities occur in mother's town, and father lives two towns away, the plan needs to address the children's activities. To change the activities in the middle of the "season" to fit the needs of the parents further penalizes the children. The plan should be written to take into account the children's schedules. In this case, the transitions may need to occur after the activities are completed on a given day, or the transition should be on a different day.

In short, you need to focus on what impact your decisions will have on the children. Will they have to carry their clothes to school? Will they have access to their things (e.g., stuffed animals, computer, favorite pillow)? Will your decision cause them to feel guilty? Will your decision pull them away from their other parent? Your conflict is not your children's, and their lives need to remain as seamless as possible.

Provides for the Right of First Refusal

High-conflict parents often fight about their right to have the children, when one of them cannot personally care for the children themselves. What happens if you cannot be with your children on one of your nights? Do you call a relative or a baby-sitter? Do you try to send your children to a friend's house? Do you think of first asking their other parent?

"I would never do that," you might say. "They wouldn't ask me. They would think I'm shirking my responsibilities. I'm not giving them more time than they already have with the children."

Imagine if you were married and one of you had to be away. You would rarely if ever consider a baby-sitter. Rather, you would expect the children to be with the other parent. That would be best for them. Why is it no longer best? It might be a bit disruptive and require a bit more communication, but shouldn't the children be with their parents whenever possible? High-conflict parents can begin to reduce conflict by showing each other consideration. A good plan is to offer each other the "right of first refusal." This means that if one of you cannot take care of the children, he or she will call the other and see if they can. If you try this strategy, do not ask for make-up time. You would not ask for such time if the children were with a baby-sitter.

Eliminates Unnecessary Transitions

High-conflict parents need to limit needless transitions. Transitions are often disruptive for children, plus they give you as parents an opportunity to needlessly engage. Even if you do not argue with each other, the children may be highly sensitive to the looks and hostile attitude you demonstrate. Some parents, for example, will not even greet each other at a transition. What does this communicate to the children? Does it show self-restraint, or does it say, "I hate your other parent so much that I won't even talk to them. This is how you are supposed to behave when you are angry with someone too"? If you can't fully control the conflict, at least limit your opportunities to engage in the battle.

The parenting plan is the cornerstone of your co-parenting relationship. Construct it well and it will serve you well. Write it with your children in mind. Make it workable. Be willing to modify it as your children's needs change. Work together on the plan. And always remember: You're doing this for the children.

CHAPTER 7

Transitions

The Trouble with Transitions

"It's that time again."

"It's time to go. I'll miss you."

"Do I have to go again, today?"

"You know when you're there I'll be thinking of you every minute."

"I can't believe it. You're late again."

"I don't want to go right now. I'm in the middle of my game."

Transitions are one of the more stressful aspects of co-parenting. They occur regularly and are grim reminders of the reality of the divorce. Transitions are opportunities for the dynamics of the divorce to be replayed over and over again. They are opportunities for the battle to continue and for payback and revenge. In conflict-addicted families, transitions are opportunities to engage. They're like the casino for the gambler and the liquor cabinet for the alcoholic.

The Drama of Good-bye

Transitions recreate separation. Once again someone is being taken away, and at least one of you doesn't want this to occur. There may be anxiety about what will happen to the child. Will they be brainwashed by "Good Time Charlie"? Will there be any consistency with what you have been trying to accomplish with the child? Will they parent as well as you do?

There may be anxiety about what will happen to the adult who is now alone. Your child may ask many questions. "Will [parent] be here when I come back?" "Will [parent] be okay while I'm away?" "Who will take care of [parent] while I'm not here?" "Will [parent] be lonely?"

Anxiety may also be fueled by the conflict the child may feel if both parents are present at the time of the transition. The child may wrestle with guilt and internal conflict about how happy he or she should be to see one parent and leave the other. This is an impossible position for a child, and it's further complicated if there has been some kind of incident that further sensitizes the child to seeing or leaving one parent. If one of you has reprimanded your child in the recent past, seeing the other parent may feel quite special to the child at that moment. Similarly, if one parent has been away, the child may be more excited to see that parent and less upset about leaving the other. These competing feelings and allegiances can cause significant anxiety.

Some children wait for days to see one parent. They may repeatedly ask, "What time is [other parent] coming?" They may wait with joyful anticipation. Other children may prepare to leave, as if they were leaving for a funeral. They know [other parent] is coming in a short time. They do not feel like going, and as the clock ticks they feel the inevitability of the moment getting closer and closer.

All of these factors can lead to rather dramatic and emotional good-byes, moments that can be heightened by the anxiety felt by the parents. You may truly miss your child when they leave. You may wonder what tricks the other parent has in store for you or your child. You may believe you are sending your child to someone who will not care for them with the same degree of skill and dedication as you would. You may dread seeing the other parent—yet again.

Your behavior may impact your child and can lead to a negative loop, which occurs when your child takes his or her cues from your behavior. This leads to an increase in their emotional distress, and then an increase in yours, and then in theirs, etc. In short, you each get more and more upset as the moment of the transition gets closer. By the time the moment arrives it as if you are sending your child away to a foreign land to return some time in the distant future. At that time, the good-bye may be heart wrenching. You may be all too glad to hear your child say, "I don't want to go. I don't feel well. My stomach hurts." Any excuse may be reason enough for you to say, "I'll call [other parent] and talk it over with them. Maybe you won't have to go today."

A Time for Remembering

"Out of sight, out of mind." We often cope with stress via denial and avoidance. You may say to yourself, "As long as I don't have to deal with [other parent], I'm okay. I could do this all myself. It would be a lot easier if they were out of the picture altogether." On a day-to-day basis, you may be pretty skilled at not thinking about your child's other parent for some time. You may go through your routine and be thoroughly entrenched in your new life.

Each transition therefore may be an assault to the serenity brought on by the denial. The transition puts you face-to-face with the failure of the marriage, with your divorce, and with that person whom you have grown to love to hate. If you see each other during the transition, there are countless reminders of the pain. Who else are they with? Who else will be taking care of your child when they aren't with you? You have to see your ex again and again. You have to see how they are dressed, the car they drive, and possibly the home in which they live. There are reminders about how they spend money, how they socialize, their attitude, and their habits.

You also see all those little habits and nuances of behavior that make them who they are. You may see a wedding band and fantasize about their wonderful new marriage. "Why couldn't they be like that with me when we were married?" you might ask. "Now they get it? I just don't understand why we couldn't have had what they have now."

Transitions can also be a time to remember the factors that contributed to the divorce. You may be reminded of all of those reasons that make you glad you're not married to this person. For example, you may come face-to-face with your memories of the events leading up to the separation. Perhaps you see them and remember one or many betrayals. You may remember the arguments or perhaps the deafening silences. Feelings of rejection may come to mind. Perhaps there are traumatic incidents that you remember.

Seeing your children's other parent can trigger these unpleasant memories, so that sending your children to be with this person can seem senseless. "Why should I have my children go with someone who has caused me (and them) so much pain? It doesn't matter that this person is their [other parent]. Look at what they've done. Who knows what will happen next? Should I expose my children to that much pain? This is ridiculous."

An Opportunity for More Disappointment and Conflict

Transitions require coordination, communication, cooperation, and consideration. When there is a breakdown in any of these areas, problems occur and again there is disappointment and potential conflict. Below is a list of some common ways in which transitions lead to disappointment. How often do these situations occur in your transitions? Have you ever contributed to these situations?

- The parent picking up the child is late.

- The parent drops the child off late.

- The child does not want to leave.

- One parent is rude, belligerent, or argumentative.

- One parent makes snide comments.

- One parent cannot even be civil.

- The children do not have enough or the right clothes.

- The children have not done their homework when with one parent.

- Clothes were sent but not returned.

There are countless other opportunities for disappointment, stemming from positive or hopeful expectations that are not met. On the other hand, each negative expectation is a self-fulfilling prophecy, causing its own problems. As you can see, conflict has a fertile breeding ground at transition times.

An Opportunity for Misunderstanding

"I thought you were coming at a quarter of six tonight," says one parent.

"No, I told you I was coming at a quarter after six," says the other parent.

"What do you mean, they have soccer practice tonight?" asks one parent.

"I told you about it last time. If you would have listened you would know," replies the other parent.

"Get away from my door!" yells one parent. "I have a restraining order and you're in violation."

"I'm simply bringing you the child. It's snowing and icy. Should I let our child slip and get hurt?" says the other.

"If you don't leave right now, I'm going to call the police," says the first parent.

Poor communication, a history of negative interactions, making assumptions, and mind reading all lead to more problems. Drama, memories, disappointment, and misunderstandings all prime the pump and fuel the conflict. Transitions are opportunities to again engage with each other. You can endlessly debate whose fault it is that one of you is late and the other early. You can point out each other's faults. You can remind each other that your old habits and criticisms are still problems. You can argue over the other's unreasonable behavior. Transitions are repeated opportunities for conflict. If you are addicted to conflict, transitions are your "fix." On certain days, some parents have two chances to "score." If your children do not have an overnight stay with the parent they're with that day, there are two transitions (a pickup and a return). From the addict's standpoint, it is like the gambler having two trips to the casino in one day. What a terrific (or is it an awful) opportunity?

A Recurring Nightmare for the Children

Unfortunately, children have to be present during transitions. They repeatedly witness the dysfunctionality of the parents. They get disappointed. They see the anger and resentment of one or both parents. They experience the old and new problems of their parents' relationship again and again. At best, they just get reminded of the divorce. At worst, they again experience the hostility and sometimes even violence of the divorce as one parent is yelling or threatening the other. It's like having the nightmare where you fall off the cliff over and over again. The circumstances may change in the dream, but the endpoint is always the same ... you're going over the cliff. Again and again the children witness the two people they love the most showing them firsthand how relationships die. They see how you hate each other and they see the resentment you have for each other. They are reminded about restraining orders. They see that their parents cannot get out of the car. They see their parents unwilling to give each other a pleasant greeting. They see their parents unable to effectively communicate and coordinate their lives. They are pawns and prisoners of their parents' old battles waged on a new frontier. They see their parents fighting, yet again.

In fact, transitions can truly be a nightmare from the children's perspective. Transitions are about the children. The entire reason there is contact between you and the other parent is because of your children; you know that, and so do your children. Your child might be thinking, "They're fighting again. I can't stand it. They're here fighting because of me. If I wasn't in the picture, they wouldn't be fighting. If they didn't have to take me back and forth, this wouldn't be happening. If I don't go back and forth, Mom and Dad won't fight. That's it! I won't go. That'll stop them from fighting. I won't go. They can't make me." At times, this self-imposed guilt can be so strong that children feel like running away. They may even become self-injurious or suicidal.

Yes, that's right. Your children might be refusing to or resisting seeing one or the other of you because the way you handle the transitions is just too painful for them. Once again, they are experiencing the pain of your conflict addiction. It evidences itself all too easily in the few moments you and the other parent are present during the transition.

Transitions and Communication

"Remember, Sally's band concert was changed. It's now Thursday night at 7:30, not Wednesday night at 7:00."

"Next Tuesday I have to work late. Can you pick the kids up, even though it's my day?"

"Tell your father the doctor changed your medicine. You are supposed to take two pills every four hours and one teaspoon of the liquid every six hours."

"Please ask your mother if it would be okay for me to bring you back late on Sunday the 15th. I'd like you to come with me to my company picnic."

"Do you have a minute? I just want to talk with you about which one of us will be taking Mark to camp."

Yes, transitions are an opportunity to have some contact with each other. There may be face-to-face contact. You may recall some of the countless details that you need to communicate. There may be questions that you would like answered. The transition feels like a way of doing this quickly. There will be little chance for prolonged interaction, so why not just send a quick message?

The problem here is that you are sending a quick message to someone with whom you have a history of poor communication and excessive conflict. You may have competing interests (or think you do) and may have little trust. These factors don't do much to heighten the likelihood that the "quick and simple message" will indeed be received accurately. Rather, it is likely that this message will be misperceived. The more conflict that is present, the more care is needed to make sure that communication is accurate and clear. Communicating on the run is likely to lead to conflict running away with the communication. In business you wouldn't carelessly communicate with someone with whom you were working on an important project (as important as your children) or with whom you are in the midst of serious conflict (for example, if you think they may be about to take you to court). Yet, parents of divorce try to do just that on a routine basis. Then they are flabbergasted that the other parent "didn't get it."

Some parents even take on the more complicated task of trying to do the business of parenting with each other at these times. They try to make a decision, solve a problem, or discuss some other situation. This is done in the presence of the child and while they are keeping the child waiting. The message to the child is, "Just wait a minute. Can't you see we're busy here?" The child may be excited (or anxious) about the transition. The transition becomes another experience where the child's needs are disregarded because their parents have "something more important" that they "have to" discuss right now. When the "discussion" breaks down, the child now sees that it is more important for the two of you to fight than to "have me go to [other parent]'s." You have again shown your child that you do not respect their needs and the agreements you have made on their behalf.

The goal of the transition is to help your children move smoothly from one parent to the other. The transition is about the children. It is not about communicating, sending messages, or doing the business of parenting with each other. If you want to sabotage the relationship and increase the conflict, then use the transition as a time to do business or take shots at each other. If you want to avoid conflict, then control your behavior during the few moments of the transition and behave in a civil manner with regard to your children and especially to your co-parent.

Guidelines for High-Conflict Parents

What Do You Mean It's Like a Pizza Delivery?

The local pizza delivery person comes to the door. They are on time and the pizza is hot. They greet you and you exchange a few pleasantries. You pay them and they depart, leaving the pizza with you. The transaction takes just one or maybe two minutes. It happens repeatedly and each time it is pretty much the same as the last time. It doesn't matter what kind of day the delivery person is having. It doesn't matter how your day is. You both come to the door with the intent of successfully completing the transaction as efficiently as possible. You both are successful virtually 100 percent of the time.

Transitioning the children from one parent to the other should run as smoothly. Children need to be transitioned on time and in an appropriate manner. There can be a structure to the transition time. It need not be negotiated anew each time. There do not need to be questions, uncertainty, or new decisions made each time. You both can be pleasant and to the point. You can accomplish the transition with ease and in a minimal amount of time.

Structuring the Transition

Be specific: When you order the pizza, you clearly communicate the size and type of pizza, your address, and when you would like the pizza delivered. The pizza restaurant communicates the price and when you can expect delivery. You are clear, they are clear, and there is no uncertainty. In fact, you may even get a free pizza if they are late! Here are a few issues to clarify regarding transitions:

- *Who* is doing the driving?

- *Where* will you meet?

- *When* will each of you get there?

- *What* other details should each parent be aware of?

The more you can keep these elements routine, the less chance there will be for misunderstanding and the breeding of conflict and distrust. Ideally, transitions should proceed the same way each time. Just like the pizza delivery, they can be on "auto-pilot," with no guesswork. It is important not to make assumptions. Be clear and make sure you can answer the four questions above. This is not rocket science. It is just specific communication.

Prepare, prepare, prepare: Preparation is often the key to a successful transition. Your children need to be ready emotionally and logistically. They need to know (and be reminded) about the transition time. They need to have the things they may be taking with them gathered. They should not be in the middle of an activity, homework, or chore. They should be fed (as appropriate) and dressed.

You too should be prepared. You need to anticipate the transition. You should make sure you are committed to avoiding conflict at that time. If you are bringing the children to the other parent, you should make sure you too are ready in a timely fashion. It is better to be a bit early rather than late. Anticipate traffic jams and other situations that may arise. If the children are coming to you, it is important to be equally ready. You should be listening for their arrival and be off the phone. Your children are entitled to a full and warm greeting when they arrive.

Consider "neutral territory": Parents often wrestle with the question of what will happen during the difficult moment when the two of you are face-to-face at the door. What if another adult (your new "friend") is visiting? What if you bought a new TV but there is an ongoing financial dispute with the other parent? What if the child does not want to leave and one or both of you begin to argue? Neutral territory avoids some of these problems. By meeting each other at a neutral spot, you preserve your privacy and you avoid that moment at the door. The children are already out of the house and in the car. The parent they are going to is not "ripping" them from what they were doing at the time and from the other parent. While inconvenient for both parents, a transition at neutral territory can be advantageous for high-conflict parents.

Such transitions usually work well if the neutral spot is easy to get to and quite visible. Often, we recommend a small retail shopping center. The parking lot at such a center (not your local mall) should be small enough that you can easily spot each other. It also affords you the opportunity to park safely while one of you is waiting for the other to arrive. The downside to neutral territory is that it may be difficult to communicate if one of you is unavoidably late (for example, due to road construction). This can be rectified with cellular telephones left on and able to receive a call. Of course, you must exchange the numbers (or at least a pager number so that you can call each other if needed).

If transitions are difficult for you, consider having them on neutral territory.

Drop-off if possible: Do you find yourself playing out scenes like these when transition time rolls around?

"Your [other parent]'s here. Get ready," says the parent. "I don't want to. I'm right in the middle of my video game," says the child.

"I don't want him/her coming to my door," says one parent. "How can I pick up the kids, if I can't knock on the door?" asks the other.

These are just two situations that high-conflict parents face. When one parent arrives at the other parent's home, the timing may be poor, even though the parent is "on time." There may be boundary issues and concern about crossing the threshold. Children may invite the other parent inside. There is more opportunity for discussion about other issues and more opportunity to argue (possibly in front of the children.)

Many parents find it less conflict inducing to drop off the child at the other parent's home. This allows the parent a bit of flexibility in making sure the child is ready to go on time. It avoids the problem of one parent waiting at the other parent's door. It doesn't put the child in the awkward position of saying good-bye to one parent in front of the other. In fact, many children can be dropped off in the driveway if they are mature enough to go inside the other parent's home or apartment on their own. The parent who is dropping off the child can say good-bye in the privacy of their own car (without the other parent right there), allow the child to walk the final distance to a nearby door, make sure the child gets inside safely, and then drive away. The child goes from the arms of one parent to those of the other without those awkward moments of feeling like they are on the bridge in the midst of a prisoner exchange in a grade "B" movie. Children are often used to being dropped off at a variety of places (such as, daycare, a friend's house, school, the movies, etc.). Dropping the child off at the other parent's home can mimic these other everyday experiences.

Talking to the Children about Transitions

The following guidelines are recommended for parents who are trying to prepare children for the parenting transitions.

Speak about the transitions in matter-of-fact terms. The transitions are not optional and should not be portrayed as such. It is important that parents demonstrate an expectancy that the child *will* go to the other parent's home. You need to communicate your support for the parenting plan just as you communicate the importance of the child going to school (even if you aren't happy with the child's teacher or the child doesn't want to go on a given day).

Support the child's relationship with your co-parent. Children need to be outside your conflict with their other parent. They need to be free to see both of you without feeling guilty or manipulated by either parent. If you support the child's relationship with the other parent by supporting the transitions, the child gets a clear message that you support having a relationship with the other parent. Unfortunately, many high-conflict parents sabotage this aspect of the family relationship. From your child's perspective because you are divorced doesn't mean that there is no longer a family. Your child still has a family (in two places) and needs this to be supported by your attitude and behavior.

Stress the importance of being on time. If you and your child are on time for the transition, you set the stage for similar action when your child is coming back to you. By focusing on being prompt, you also communicate the importance you place on the child's relationship with the other parent. Finally, you teach the child about the general importance of being on time.

Let the child know you will be okay. Children need to be able to transition without excessive worry. Do not repeatedly tell the child you will miss them and that you are worrying about them. You inadvertently put them in the role of the parent and cause them worry and guilt about leaving you to see their other parent. Imagine the impossible situation for the child if both parents put the child in this position.

Remind the child shortly before the transition time. Children get involved in the activity of the moment. As the time to leave for the transition approaches, it is often useful to remind the child to get ready to go. This can help them take a moment to prepare emotionally so they can then can finish the current activity in a timely manner.

Encourage the child to enjoy their time with their other parent. Too often, children complain that they feel like "luggage." Parents act as if they are just transporting their children, and fail to communicate their caring for the child. While children should not generally be given the message that they are going to "visit" a parent, they should be encouraged to enjoy their time with the other parent. They do not need to feel like they have to hide having a "good time" in their other home.

Talking to the Other Parent during Transitions

Keep it simple. Transitions are not times to do business. Keep your conversation simple and to the point. Do not discuss any issues. Absolutely do *not* argue.

Confirm the next transition. Parents sometimes find it helpful to confirm the next transition time. It can be helpful to verify that nothing has changed and that there are no special exceptions. This can be especially important if the current transition involves a modification of time or place. Make sure you are back to the normal routine and make sure you have discussed who will be where. The authors have seen parents leave their child at school, both being convinced that the other was going to pick up the child.

Cordial and pleasant greetings are just fine. Greet the other parent with at least as much cordiality as you would greet a stranger or a baby-sitter. Demonstrate the level of respect that you would want to see from the other parent. Demonstrate the same manners and respect in front of your children that you would want them to demonstrate to you. *You* are the role model. You need to *do* the right thing, even if you do not *feel* the right thing.

The following simple script may be useful. You can modify it to fit your own style. Notice how uncomplicated and basic the discussion is and how at the same time it avoids opportunity for conflict. In this particular example the Second Parent is bringing the child to the First Parent.

First Parent: "Hi [name of second parent]. Hi [name of child]."

Second Parent: "Hi [name of first parent]."

First Parent: "How are you?"

Second Parent: "Fine. How are you?"

First Parent: "Okay."

Second Parent: "[name of child] has an ear infection. His medicine and the directions are in this bag. His next dose is due at [time]."

First Parent: "No problem. Is there anything else I need to know about his ears?"

Second Parent: "No. That's about it. He had a bit of a temperature yesterday, but seems fine now."

First Parent: "Okay, then. I'll drop him off at your house on [day] at [time]."

Second Parent: "That's fine. I'll be there."

First Parent: "I'll see you then. [Child's name] say good-bye to [parent]."

Second Parent: "Bye-bye. See you [day]."

This conversation conveys only the necessary information. It avoids problem solving and conflict and confirms the arrangements for the next transition. It also supports the relationship the child has with each parent. The child is encouraged to say good-bye to the parent he is leaving. This discussion is centered on the needs of the child and does not involve the parents in other (e.g., financial) matters.

There are no overt or subtle exchanges of resentment or hostility. This same conversation (or one close to it) could happen time and time again, making the transitions routine, uneventful, and most certainly not scary for the child.

Reschedule detailed discussions until your parenting phone call. Do not try to do the business of parenting on the run at a transition. If the other parent brings up something that needs attention and time to discuss, politely suggest that it be put high on the agenda for your upcoming parenting call. High-conflict parents do not communicate well, even if there is time. They certainly do not communicate well on the run and in front of children who may be emotional (angry, excited, scared, sad) about the transition.

Changing Plans at the Last Minute

In a word, don't. You need your credibility. Credibility is built over time and with consistency and predictability. Frequent changes and last-minute changes erode credibility. These changes also can be quite confusing for the children. Such changes are open to misinterpretation because high-conflict parents are experts at attributing motives to the behavior of the other parent.

> *"You were late just to get back at me for reminding you that you didn't send the last child support payment."*

> *"You asked for that change just to make my life more difficult."*

> *"You said you couldn't bring the kids back on time just to make me look like a *!@^& for wanting them here at the time agreed to in our parenting plan."*

High-conflict parents need the structure of a parenting plan. If you change this structure frequently, the structure becomes meaningless and your "agreement" becomes meaningless. In business you wouldn't contract with a client, only to repeatedly change the contract, and then change it again. High-conflict parenting is like having your best client also be your most difficult client. Your business depends on this client, yet they are difficult to manage. You wouldn't add to the difficulty by changing an already agreed-upon contract, so don't do that with your co-parent. You need a consistent structure to your interactions.

Transitioning as Co-Parents

You have a wonderful opportunity at the time of each transition. It is a time to show your children that together as parents you love your children more than you love fighting with each other. Transitions are times when you can routinely show your children that parents can work together. You can communicate by your actions that even though a marriage may fall apart, parents can still be parents and not exes. You can show your children that you have their interests at heart. You can show them that you respect their feelings and their love for *both* their parents. This is a wonderful opportunity. You can show your children that their parents can be respectful and adult and do the right thing, in spite of the sadness of a divorce. You teach them that it is possible to manage hurt and emotional turmoil on a prolonged basis. You teach them that they too can manage their feelings in their relationships throughout life. If you act like an adult (not a warrior or victim) you teach your children a wonderful lesson and give them a tremendous opportunity to love you both and freely go from one of you to the other without guilt and with minimal anxiety. You will give your children a chance to have a more normal experience and not relive the divorce each time they go from one of you to the other.

Transitions are opportunities for conflict or opportunities for life lessons. It's your choice. Build cooperation, build normalcy, and build collaboration. It is up to you to use your transitions well.

Chapter 8

Discipline

Disciplinary Differences

Imagine for a moment you are not divorced or separated. You and your partner are raising your children together. As your children grow, there are countless situations that develop and challenge your resources as parents. Do you take a stand to teach a particular moral or value in a specific instance? When your child misbehaves, do you say nothing or do you take away a privilege? Do you punish the child? How severe is your reaction going to be? How consistent should you be? Should you change your mind after you have grounded your child for "the rest of your life!"?

These are a few of the many questions with which parents wrestle. In an intact family, parents accept that they don't have all the answers. They seek input from each other, friends, professionals, and extended family members. They read books and magazines and they listen to radio and television shows searching for the magic answers that will guide them in helping mold their children into happy, responsible, and successful adults.

High-conflict parents often struggle over control. They struggle to protect their interests and their role as a parent. They struggle to prove that they have what it takes to be a competent and loving parent. They often attack the other parent to defend their own position and to keep the heat off themselves. In high-conflict divorces, it seems that often at least one parent immediately becomes an "expert," clearly believing that he or she knows what's best. The other parent, by default, becomes virtually incompetent in the mind of the first parent. Of course, this dynamic can happen simultaneously to both parents, giving the child two "experts" and two incompetent parents (depending on who is being asked). Yet, raising your child didn't become easier following the divorce. In fact, it has become more difficult in many respects. There are more stress, confusion, conflict, and complications. The logistics are more difficult and communication is more difficult. Moreover, your child is dealing with the divorce on a daily basis and may now have more needs than if the family remained intact.

Additionally, high-conflict divorced families face many of these stresses and additional difficulties:

- Vastly differing views about parenting

- Excessive control battles between the parents

- Children who are seeking extra attention from one or both parents

- A tendency to blame one another for the behavior they see in the children

- A propensity toward additional litigation and multiple (and often trivial) changes in the parenting plan

- The impact of new relationships and stepfamilies

- Conflict that is fueled by well-meaning friends and extended family members who say, "You're going to go along (or let them get away) with that?"

- Financial stresses

- Moves, plus lifestyle and career changes

Parenting professionals will often say, "There is no one right answer. There are a number of ways you can handle that situation." This doesn't change after a divorce. You and your children's other parent do not hold the magic answers. Your children need the benefit of the wisdom and insight of both parents. They need the best that you *both* have to offer. They don't need the best of one of you and none of the rest. Why should they get less because their parents are divorced?

You also need your co-parent. They are with your child for approximately one-third to two-thirds of the time. If they cannot give you useful ideas, you still need them to be involved so they do not undermine and sabotage your plans. You may believe they would do this just to get back at you, but in our experience most parents are able to recognize that their children need to be effectively parented, in spite of each parent's feelings toward the other. Do you want input? Do you want to be involved? Does your child need two parents who communicate and coordinate their discipline (and rewards)? You bet they do! Yet, high-conflict parents will often answer "no" to these questions. They often are convinced they can do it better alone. They believe if they just had the power and the control, their children would be fine. Even if you have a high-conflict co-parenting relationship, you need to work together. If you don't work together, your children will experience the two of you working apart. In the corporate world, this would be like reporting to two supervisors who each had different work objectives, strategic plans, values, and missions. Just as it would drive you crazy to work in such an environment, it will probably do the same to your children.

Agreeing on Basic Values

In our offices we see high-conflict parents fight over each other's actions. They argue about each other's motives and do not stop to recognize areas of agreement. You cannot possibly discuss and agree on every decision you each will make as parents. However, if you agree on basic values, these can be a shared guide for many different parenting decisions. By agreeing on values, you can get to the same endpoint even when you make different decisions or when you take different parenting paths. It is like charting a number of sailing courses, all toward the same shore.

You might find it helpful for you and your co-parent to independently take the following survey and see how many items you actually agree on. Simply answer each item True or False.

_____ We should avoid physical punishments.

_____ On school nights our children should go to sleep at a specific time.

_____ Our children should go to school unless they are clearly ill.

___ Our children should do their homework and study on a routine basis.

___ As parents, we should help them with their studies.

___ Our children should be rewarded by us for their accomplishments.

___ Our children should be taught good moral values.

___ We should not allow our children to do dangerous things.

___ Our children need to understand about being responsible to others.

___ Our children should have chores appropriate for their ages and abilities.

___ When disciplining our children, the punishment should fit the crime.

In high-conflict families, the parents don't see each other's strengths. High-conflict parents put most of their energies into fighting about things about which they cannot agree. They also expect that they should agree about most things and do not value the areas where agreement is already in place. As parents, you can build from each of your strengths. You need to assume that each of you has something to offer the children. Instead of fighting about your disagreements, make decisions that support your common values. Get used to collaborating where it is easy to do so. Make collaboration a habit in some areas. It may become contagious and spread to other areas later.

A Case Example

Two parents who were never married had a teenage daughter who was spending excessive time on the Internet. Her grades were falling. Her friends also started visiting without permission when she was at her mother's and Mom was at work. These friends got into some mischief and also visited Web sites that were inappropriate for teenagers. Her parents discussed the situation and agreed that their daughter would not be allowed to use the Internet in either household for a period of two weeks. They would each take the computer cable. They agreed that if the daughter was caught having friends over when mom was at work, then she would not be allowed to stay home alone and would have to go to father's after school until mother returned from work. They spoke to their daughter about this plan together and made the consequences clear without arguing among themselves.

Separate Houses, Separate Discipline

Parents who are addicted to conflict often feel sabotaged by their co-parent when, after initiating a consequence for discipline, they find that the other parent did not support it in the other home. In fact, they often feel the other parent deliberately undermined them. We often hear, "[Other parent] let [child] play video games even though I prohibited it, just to get back at me. [Other parent] does not care at all about the impact of his/her actions on our child. It's all about getting back at me and taking control." Yet, why would we expect that if parents have a conflict-based relationship, they would be able to effectively co-parent when it comes to the complex set of decisions around discipline? If the simple decisions are difficult, the complex decisions are likely to be nearly impossible.

It is clearly preferable for conflict-addicted parents to work together (such as in the above case example) when it comes to discipline. We have seen children essentially "fall out of their socks" when both parents sit down with them to discuss an incident and the consequences that "we, your parents, have decided together." This message shows the children that you mean business. It says, "This situation is so important to us that we have put aside our differences and are telling you together what needs to be done." If you work together, discuss the situation, don't blame each other, decide on a course of action, and then both follow through on this course, you have given your child the benefit of the combined strength of both parents.

Unfortunately, this level of collaborative co-parenting is too tall an order for many parents who are in high-conflict relationships. They easily get off track and do not jointly support each other. In these cases, it is often advisable to initiate discipline that does not require cooperation by the other parent. This may require you to be a bit more creative and also to recognize that whatever you put in place may not be followed in the child's other home.

Control the Privileges the Child Has While He/She Is with You

Restrictions of such privileges can extend beyond the child's current time with you and carry over to when they return to your home. For example, if you are using grounding as a punishment, you can make it clear that not going out for two weekends means not going out for the next two weekends that the child is with you. You can curtail television or Internet privileges or have earlier bedtimes on the nights the child is in your home.

Require That Certain Chores Be Done While the Child Is with You

An unpleasant chore can become the consequence for an inappropriate behavior. It is best to be clear about the level, duration, and extent of the consequence. You can, for example, make it clear that you expect the chore to be done for each day this week that the child is in your home.

Ideally, you and your co-parent should work to agree on consequences. But, with high-conflict parents, it may be necessary to compartmentalize the discipline to your own home. This way you don't have to reach agreement on the reasonableness of the consequence and on the follow-through of the consequence.

The Importance of Consistency

Parents from intact families have difficulty parenting in a relatively consistent fashion. They establish consequences (positive and negative) and only follow through for a short time. They change their mind about consequences that seemed right at the time but now seem too harsh. They begin homework programs and home behavioral modification programs only to have their own energies erode so that they fail to follow through. All this happens with two parents in the home who can support one another and pick up when the other parent has difficulty.

Many divorced parents are unfortunately—and needlessly—functioning as single parents. They don't have the support of another adult, and in high-conflict divorces they may perceive that the other parent ridicules them and undermines their actions. This is an added burden and naturally makes parenting even more demanding. To further complicate matters, parents who are divorced often are coping with their own emotional reactions. You may feel depressed, have less energy, experience decreased concentration, and be distracted by all the legalities and practical problems you face. This is even more often the case for parents who are in high-conflict divorces.

At the same time, a child in a divorced family often hears more inconsistent messages. The world may be more confusing for this child. What is true in one home is not true in the other. For example, in mom's house the child is taught that his/her bed must be made in the morning. In dad's house this is not the case, but dad requires help with certain household tasks while mom does not have these same requirements. It can be a bit more difficult for the child to know what's "right." If there is also a great deal of inconsistency within each home, the world can appear even more confusing. This can be especially true for young children who are first trying to learn the rules, and for adolescents who are at the developmental stage where they are in the process of challenging the rules.

If you as co-parents can be consistent (without being unduly rigid), you can help your child learn that there are some values, principles, and expectations that are important. You can help your child learn that there are times when you mean business and that what you say counts. If both parents give the child the same message, you are adding more emphasis to the point in the child's experience.

Remember that consistency is not just related to what you say. It is demonstrated by what you do as well. If you set an expectation that you will, for example, go to church regularly, take the child out for pizza if they do well on a test in school, increase their allowance if they do an extra chore, and then do not follow through, you are communicating that your word is not something they can count on. You diminish your credibility. Follow-through is important for parents living in intact families. It is more important for parents of divorce and is even more important for parents in high-conflict divorces.

Shooting First and Asking Questions Later

Your child comes back from being with their other parent for the weekend. They walk in the door with red and teary eyes and are looking rather forlorn. You say, "Is everything all right?" and they begin to tell you how your co-parent has been mean and unreasonable. "Well, well," you think, "now I have some grist for the mill. [Other parent] is finally going to get his/her just desserts." You respond to your child by supporting their feelings. "I can't understand why [other parent] would do that," you say. "It doesn't make any sense to me. I'm sorry this had to happen to you." You reach for the phone or fire a quick and scalding e-mail message. Your reaction is impulsive and instantaneous.

Are you taking this approach because you believe the child? Is this a chance for you to get back at the other parent for past assaults on you? Is this an opportunity for you to gain points with your child by siding with the child?

How do you handle complaints in other relationships when one person complains to you about another? Do you immediately take a stand or do you stop and seek out more information to make sure you have the complete picture? Unfortunately, high-conflict parents often shoot first. They assume the worst and do not believe that their co-parent might actually be justified. It is possible that they were not being as "mean and unreasonable" as the child perceived or portrayed. It is quite possible that the other parent was behaving reasonably. Your children may not be the best interpreters of parental motivations and behaviors. They know how to stir things up, especially when struggling with the intense loyalty conflicts imposed by high-conflict parents. Your assumption needs to be that your co-parent cares about your children and tries to discipline them within reason. Don't you want them to make the same assumptions about you?

If you can ask your co-parent questions first (in a non-threatening manner), you may generally do better than if you hold court, judge, and then convict them based on your child's comments.

Sample questions for co-parents when talking to each other about what the children have said happened at the other parent's house:

- "[Child] mentioned to me that [incident] happened. Can you tell me about it?"

- "[Child] seemed upset yesterday when he came home. He mentioned he was punished when he was with you. What happened? Is there anything I can do to help support you?"

- "I just heard from [child] about what happened yesterday. What he said sounded somewhat incredible. I'd really like to get the story straight from you so I can better know how I should deal with him."

Making a Choice about Collaboration

One child and two parents automatically equals a triangle for interactions. Divorced parents with conflict do not necessarily feel predisposed to work together. They make the triangle more pronounced. You may say, "I've tried, but what has it gotten me? The more I give, the more I continue to be disappointed, or even beaten up emotionally."

In short, you have three choices when it comes to discipline and dealing with your child's other parent. You can resist their attempts at discipline, sabotage their attempts, or collaborate with them. The odds are not particularly good here because you each have three options, and there is only one combination that will pay off: collaboration by both parents. To make matters worse, you only have control over one of the two parties—you. In all likelihood, you have tried to be collaborative. You have tried to listen and not be judgmental. You have tried to include the other parent in your decisions with regard to discipline. You may be saying, "Yeah, I've tried, and what has it gotten me? Every time I try, I get kicked in the teeth. I cannot collaborate. I have to do my own thing." You may decide to try to avoid sabotage, yet how can you when you do not actively and routinely communicate a desire to collaborate?

It is important to strive to collaborate and then strive again and again. If you give up in this regard, you are in some sense giving up on your child. You are taking a position that says, "It's just too hard. It just won't work. I might as well accept the status quo even though that's not what's best for my child." If you and your co-parent both resign yourselves to this position, it is unlikely things will ever improve. You allow the status quo to become the norm, and you build a habit of not collaborating about your child. On the other hand, if you keep seeking collaboration, you might just get through to your co-parent. Maybe you will get through to them some of the time. Perhaps there will be an inkling of success on one occasion that can be the beginning of slowly achieving future successes. Seek collaboration and then seek it again and again. You need to make the decision that pursuing collaboration is so much more important than pursuing the conflict.

Guidelines for Discussing Discipline

As you seek collaboration about discipline, it can be quite useful to keep in mind the following guidelines:

Avoid Accusatory Tones

"I just heard that you really had a problem with [child]. What happened this time?"

"[Child] said that you disciplined him for [incident]. I can't believe you took that approach for something like that. What were you thinking?"

When your comments indicate that you assume your co-parent has again been an incompetent parent, you are fostering more conflict. As soon as you begin to sound like you are making an accusation, it is highly likely that your co-parent will either become defensive or make a counterattack that will involve accusing you of some other offense. Be sure to speak calmly and in a nonjudgmental fashion. If you begin with an accusation, you communicate that you have found the other parent "guilty" without getting all the information. You also can be perceived as being disinterested in solving a problem and more interested in using the situation against your co-parent.

Get the Basic Information

Your five-year-old comes home and says, "Daddy, Daddy . . . Mommy hit me! She's mean." "What happened?" you say. Your child continues, "I was playing outside with [sibling] and Mommy yelled at me and hurt me." Your child can only give you his or her perception of the situation. This view is distorted by your child's level of maturity and perspective. What went on here? Is the mother in this example acting unreasonably? How would you feel if your child came home and told you the same thing? What would you think? Do you really know the circumstances? Upon questioning the other parent, you might find that the child was running toward the street to chase a ball. The parent used a minimum amount of physical influence (grabbed the child by the arm) and did indeed speak sternly to the child. If you do not get the basic information first, and only listen to your child, you could easily (as many parents do) assume that the other parent's behavior may be quite unreasonable or even abusive.

Seek Input on Difficult Situations

Your fourteen-year-old is being disrespectful. Lectures and threats do not work. You ask the child if he or she speaks to their other parent in the same way. They say, "Well, no." You ask, "Then why do you think it's okay to talk to me like that?" Your child then shrugs and walks away. How would you feel in this situation? It is likely that you'd feel some combination of anger, frustration, self-doubt, jealousy of your co-parent's abilities to parent your child, and a sense that you might be losing this relationship as you lost the relationship with your co-parent. You might feel quite alone at that moment.

But you are not alone. Your co-parent may have dealt with the same situation in the past, or may have to deal with it in the near future. At times, we find that one parent has developed a strategy that seems to work rather well with a child in a particular situation. The other parent may have techniques that work equally well for other situations. If you seek input from each other you have the opportunity to exchange this information. Imagine if two business partners (e.g., in sales, professional service, product development, or construction) didn't get input from each other. How successful would the business be? Your children need the benefit of the strengths of both parents. If you were married, you would combine efforts. Your children should get this same benefit now. Ask for the help you need.

In the above example, you could say to the other parent, "I'm having some trouble with [child] lately. I know he is fourteen and he has been through a lot, but he doesn't seem to show me any respect. Is he ever that way with you? How do you handle him when he starts to get this way?" By asking the question, you may get useful information. You set the stage to begin collaborating by communicating to the other parent that they actually might have some value. Too often parents feel they are superfluous to the other parent and that their efforts and insights are not valued. Asking for some needed input can help communicate a desire to collaborate and a recognition of the value of the other parent. Who knows, they might start to ask for your input on other matters.

Kindly Offer Suggestions

When asked for input, give it kindly. Remember, you are being asked for input, not a directive. You do not have a position of authority over the other parent. How would you feel if your co-parent told you what to do? Would your initial reaction be to comply or more likely to resist? When asked for input you have a wonderful opportunity to have some influence if you deliver your message carefully, with tact and kindness. It can be helpful to give the input in a way that also clearly affirms your recognition that your co-parent is trying their best and that you appreciate the chance to possibly be of help. The request for input is what you want to reinforce. It is even more important than the outcome of the specific situation. Building the collaborative co-parenting relationship is more crucial than whether your input is followed on one occasion.

Imagine two different answers to the situation with the fourteen-year-old:

Answer #1: "I don't know. He's never that way with me. You must be too lenient. Or maybe you're treating him the same way you treated me. You're blowing that relationship too. I don't know why you're surprised."

Answer #2: "Fourteen-year-olds can be really difficult. I don't find that he's too bad with me in terms of respect. Sometimes he starts to go off on me, but I find that if I quickly give him a warning and then take something away, like his telephone or computer time, if he doesn't shape up, then he seems to come back to earth. Right now, I think he needs to see that we mean business and just won't tolerate his baloney. You know, I appreciate you asking. This stuff can be really hard."

You are in control of which answer you give. You don't have to feel good about the other parent to say Answer #2. You might give an answer with a similar tone to someone in business or to an acquaintance. You can answer the question in a number of different ways. You can fuel the conflict by getting off the subject or by refusing to offer useful information, or you can address the problem in a way that lessens the conflict. It's up to you.

It's Tough but Worth It

Collaborating about discipline is one of the most important—and most challenging—demands on co-parents. It requires communication, a sharing of information, follow-through, and a willingness to see yourselves as a team, while recognizing the limits of the co-parent relationship. Although it is challenging, it is truly in the best interests of your children. Remember, it's not about you or your co-parent—it's only to benefit your child. When high-conflict parents do not attend to the need to coordinate around discipline, they are inevitably giving their children the message that rules really do not matter. They teach their children how to disrespect authority and that the world is not a place that functions in a somewhat uniform manner. They do not teach their children common values. This is perhaps one of the more damaging consequences of conflict addiction. If you insist within yourself on collaborating around discipline, you can begin to focus on providing some level of stability for your child across households.

CHAPTER 9

Activities and Special Events

Co-Parenting at Special Events

The busy lives of children continue even after the divorce. How should you handle these activities and events? Should you both go, or just the parent who has the children that night? How will you handle seeing the other parent and seeing his or her new spouse? Clearly, there are many emotionally charged issues that surround these events. Parents need to learn how to manage their feelings as well as the logistics, so they don't miss the wonderful moments in the lives of their children.

It is important to remember that the goal at these times is to be there for your children. You want to continue to participate in all aspects of your children's lives and you certainly do not want to be left out of the special times. This may mean having to cope directly with the other parent before, during, and after these special times and activities. High-conflict parents have a particularly difficult time co-parenting nicely when they are actually in each other's presence. Old feelings arise easily and may take over all your good attempts to control old behaviors. Parents lose sight of the children and return to their depressed, angry, and agitated selves. They lose sight of the real goal of attending these events, which is to make sure that your child has the love and support of both parents and extended family at these important moments.

Cordiality is the key word in co-parenting during activities and events. This is not a time to compete for the attention of your child. It is not a time for trying to win the award for "best" parent. Remember, it's a time for the child to perform for those around him or her and feel the accomplishment of doing a good job. Your child does not need to be distracted by your anger or your need to prove that the other parent is not as good or as consistent a parent as you believe yourself to be. Events and activities, like transition times, often become chances to exchange looks, jibes, sarcastic remarks, money, or information. High-conflict parents are talented at using every opportunity to get back at the other parent. These meetings are often a breeding ground for a return to behaviors that will only increase the level of animosity.

Special events are times in which parents should enjoy watching their children perform, achieve a milestone, reach a goal, or move through some developmental phase. Unfortunately, they are also times in which old memories of family and plans once held for the future painfully come to the surface. Parents remember how they anticipated these moments and how they talked about them from the day that their children were born and even before. The pictures that they painted will not be realized after all. At these times parents tend to feel a profound sense of loss and disappointment that is often expressed in ways that look like anything but sadness. Conflict becomes the prime expression of their emotional discomfort.

Expectations of High-Conflict Parents

Most high-conflict parents approach events and activities with trepidation because they anticipate unpleasant behaviors by the other parent. They expect to be ignored, shunned, and rejected by their co-parent. They weigh the joy that they will experience via participating in the lives of their children at these times with the discomfort that they will feel seeing or even sitting with the other parent. They worry, plan, and discuss the possibilities with sympathetic friends. Unfortunately, the children, who need to be exempt from all their parents' leftover hostility, are exposed to this anxiety. Like their parents, they expect some sort of unpleasant behavior. And the parents and children aren't the only ones: The extended family, friends, teachers, coaches, and others also approach these times with uncertainty. This apprehension on all parts contributes to conflict, in some cases making it inevitable.

Events and Activities— A Lifelong List

If you think that your co-parenting appearances at the events and activities of your children end somewhere after the high school years, you're wrong! This is a lifelong project that extends beyond your children to grandchildren and maybe great-grandchildren. That's why it is imperative that you make it a habit to put aside your differences for the sake of your children at these special times. There are many times you may be called upon to come together for the children, and there are many decisions that must be made concerning these types of events. Following are a few questions to consider.

When special events or activities occur . . .

- Do you both attend?

- Who comes with you?

- Who brings the child to the event or activity?

- Do you sit with the other parent or not?

- What do you both do after the event or activity?

- What do you say to the child before the event or activity about your co-parenting?

On special occasions . . .

- Do you have a joint party?

- Do you split the day?

- Do you celebrate on different days (keeping to the parenting plan)?

- Who plans the party?

- How are the invitations addressed?

At those unfortunate times when trauma occurs . . .

- How and when do you notify each other?

- How will you conduct yourselves in the presence of your child and others?

- How will you decide about consulting professionals?

- Who will stay with the child?

- Who will notify the child or other children?

- How will information be exchanged?

- Will you make decisions together or not?

A List of Possible Events

There are many, many types of events and activities that require parents to cooperate and come together for the sake of the children. Some of these are specific to your particular family, but others are relatively generic. Here is an extensive but not exhaustive list of some of these pertinent times.

Family Occasions

- Birthdays

- Holidays

- Religious milestones

- Weddings

- Births and milestones of grandchildren

School-Related Activities

- Parent conferences

- Performances

- Parent association meetings

- Open houses

- Special parent/child events (picnics, family nights, etc.)

- Graduations

- College trips

Activities

- Sports practices and games

- Music, dance, and other lessons

- Recitals

- Award dinners

- End of season parent/child parties

- Weekend and overnight trips for teams and/or other activities

- Tryouts

Traumas

- Children's illnesses

- Parent's illnesses

- Accidents

- Deaths of friends and extended family

Not all the items on this list are equally problematic for all co-parents. But in general, high-conflict parents have difficulty with a much higher percentage of these events, and they aren't always aware of the effect of their behavior on their children. They tend to be unprepared, impulsive, and unable to control their responses, even at some of these special times. Their conflict addiction is so strong that they cannot seem to turn down any opportunity to reengage the other parent in the old battles. Of course, these times also necessitate planning together, perhaps being together, and coping with extended family. This increases the proportion of direct contact with each other exponentially. Remember that everyone else is also watching both of you. This is *not* a time for a theatrical performance aimed at winning alliances! Your children are the only important ones in your audience.

Structuring Events and Activities

Preparation

The key to successful co-parenting at these special but sometimes stressful times is a lot of advance preparation. Being prepared takes time and requires the exchange of information. Warning: A laissez-faire attitude increases the chance of a conflictual interaction. Instead of being casual about it, think about your and your co-parent's potential behavior *before* the event. Figure out the potential pitfalls so you can avoid them. Preparation generally means reliable, informative, and honest communication. Obviously, this is extremely difficult for high-conflict parents. These times present an opportunity to withhold details, act out, and try to win children over to their side.

What Needs to Be Communicated?

Do not make assumptions about the amount and type of information that needs to be communicated. High-conflict parents usually have little direct interaction with one another, so they don't focus on being informative. Of course, the only ones who lose out when a parent is late or gets the time mixed up are the children. They don't care who got the schedule wrong or who didn't tell the other parent. They only know that one of the parents missed the game or did not show up to watch the pageant. Is the disappointment of the child or the hurt that they experience worth "winning" over the other parent? The list below may seem simple, but many parents forget that this important information needs to be exchanged for successful co-parenting during special times and activities:

1. The date and times of the events and all preceding practices

2. Where specifically will the event or activity take place? If there is more than one date, will the activity always be held in the same place?

3. Who is in charge—teacher, coach, other parent, etc.—and how is this person best reached?

4. What is the program? Or, what is the general procedure for lessons, practices, etc.?

5. How will transportation be provided? Is the parent who is responsible that day and time going to take care of transport, or will other arrangements need to be made?

6. What are the telephone numbers needed to secure information in case of possible cancellation or a change in plans?

7. Is there going to be a cost? If so, what is it and will it be divided between the parents? If not, who will pay? To whom should payment be made and when is it due?

8. Are there special clothing requirements? If so, what are they? How will uniforms, costumes, or clothes for specific activities (sport shoes, bathing suit, etc.) be exchanged when children are going back and forth between homes?

9. Are there equipment requirements? If so, what are they and how are they going to be exchanged?

10. Who will be going to the event or activity? Will extended family be coming? Will siblings be coming, and if so, with whom? Will new significant others be coming? Will new spouses and new siblings be coming?

11. Where will everyone sit? Do you plan to sit together or not? Will siblings sit with one parent or the other? Will that be their choice or up to the parents?

12. Will the other parent (and family) have the opportunity to see the child before the event or activity? Will the other parent (and family) have the opportunity to see the child after the event or activity?

13. How will everyone be expected to behave before, during, and after the event or activity?

14. What will be communicated to the children concerning your preparation and decisions about all of the above?

Discussion of the above points should take place well before the event or activity is supposed to occur. It is always better to provide extensive detail, even what seems like excessive information. What you think is too much probably is not. Details are very helpful in avoiding conflict. Since high-conflict parents don't like to talk with one another, they will frequently leave out pieces of information that would be very helpful at securing a smooth process. They also leave out information so that the other parent has to "work at it." As one parent put it, "Why should I have to provide all the information? If he has suddenly become such an interested parent, then he should get it himself. What am I, his secretary?" The point here is well taken, but often one parent does have access to more information (friends, schools, teams, and coordinators of extracurricular activities may prefer to just send the information to one address). If a practice or lesson is changed or canceled, then that call will often go to just one phone number. Since high-conflict parents often do not like to listen, they also miss the essential details. You both need to stay fully informed, and you need each other's help to do that. Communicating important and necessary information by writing or e-mail can also be helpful to avoid confusion. Remember your child's disappointed, hurt, or embarrassed face. Is it worth it?

No Surprises, Please

Most of the above information can be exchanged during a structured parenting communication time. The parent phone call discussed in chapter 5 is a perfect opportunity for this discussion. As you may recall, the phone call agenda included a section on activities and scheduling. The logistics and the discussion of behavioral expectations can also help make the event or activity go smoothly, with no conflict. Surprises are not welcome or useful, so don't just show up at these times without advance notice to the other parent. You both may agree that you can attend all events and activities, but you need to set standards for your behavior right from the start. Also, be sure to notify the other parent if you will be bringing a significant other or extended family to an event.

Case Example

In one case a father brought his new and visibly pregnant wife to the children's elementary school open house without telling his co-parent first. The mother was hurt and confused and unable to contain her emotions, even in this public setting. The father's behavior unfortunately felt like a breach of trust. In addition, the parents had agreed to attend the individual children's parent conferences together. These were to be scheduled at the time of the open house. The mother was instead informed that the father and his new wife now planned to attend these conferences together and that the mother could schedule her own meeting times.

Another surprise! This resulted in a loud and relationship-damaging exchange between the father, the new wife, and the mother. For a long time, it interfered significantly with all attempts at cooperative co-parenting. The relationship was only repaired after direct intervention in our P.E.A.C.E. Program. This included meetings with both parents where we discussed the impact of their conflict on the children. They had to agree to change their behavior and to set up a structure for future communication about events and activities. The meetings also included one joint session attended by the father's new wife, the father, and the mother. At that time, they all agreed to abide by some rules of interaction when in the presence of the children. From then on, all parents were expected to discuss any proposed changes to agreed-upon procedures ahead of time. They also agreed to interact cordially and decently at all events and activities with or concerning the children.

Just remember that old adage, "An ounce of prevention is worth a pound of cure."

Guidelines for Parents

The behaviors expected at these times are not really any different than those expected at all times that parents are in the presence of the children or acting in relation to the children. But high-conflict parents are the first to forget their manners at these times. They regress to acting in rude and unacceptable ways that would not be tolerated in any other relationship in their lives. For some reason they cannot refrain from using the opportunity to take a shot at the other parent. Why waste the chance? In addition, these times present unique circumstances in which parents and sometimes extended family and friends may come together for longer periods of time than transition moments require. This gives conflict a greater breeding ground and more concentrated time in which to develop. Therefore, co-parents must be even better prepared, more alert to pre-conflict signals, and in tighter control of their behavior.

How should parents act in front of their audience at these times of special events and activities?

- Parents should be cordial.

- Parents should be polite.

- Parents should be able to have a basic conversation.

- Parents should stay focused on their children and not on themselves.

- Parents should arrive on time and leave on time.

- Parents should look cheerful, pleasant, and proud in front of the children. They should not wear their negative emotions on their sleeves.

What behaviors should be avoided at these times of special events and activities?

- Parents should not engage in any substantive conversations with each other. Save those for your parenting call.

- Parents should not try to work out even simple scheduling changes, etc.

- Parents should not compete for the attention of their children. This includes the child who is engaging in the event or activity and their siblings who may be attending.

- Parents should not refer to any old issues or continue any unfinished discussions.

- Parents should not prohibit siblings, family, or friends from interacting with the other parent and/or family.

- Parents should not prevent the other parent from being able to interact with the child who is involved either before or after the event or activity.

The main goal here is to make sure that your child and their siblings do not have to experience your discomfort. They do not need to be exposed to your continued anger, distrust, and hurt—especially at these times. They need your support, want you both there (if you can act like adults), and do not need the distraction of your parenting issues. If you do not agree to act in a manner that will make your children comfortable with seeing you together, then your only choice is to miss out on at least some of these times. It's wrong to subject your children to more conflict. Either get along, or stay home. Who loses then?

More Case Examples

Parents Who Didn't Follow the Rules

The Soccer Game

Bob and Pat have three children, all in elementary school. Their oldest son plays soccer, which involves practices and weekend games. They have an alternating schedule on weekends. Both parents agreed that, within reason, they should be able to attend these activities. Bob has remarried and Pat has not. Bob often attends these activities with his new wife. Pat attends almost all of the children's activities and practices. Therefore, Pat very often sees the children on Bob's weekends. Bob does not usually attend their activities on "Pat's time" with the children, except for games and/or special events. He believes that Pat should do the same and resents the fact that she shows up at these activities and sometimes even sits with their other children, who come to watch their sibling. In fact, he has even prohibited the siblings from going over to the bleachers to sit with Mom. They barely address each other, and Pat and Bob's new wife hardly speak at all. The hostility flows freely at these times.

It is very important for Bob and Pat to understand that they should both have permission to attend the children's events and activities. Yet it is also important for Pat to realize that she does not have to be there for every single moment of the children's lives. This is such a hard concept for divorced parents to comprehend. You can't always be with the children, at least not as often as you would like, or as often as prior to the divorce. The only way to maximize your time is to cooperate with the other parent. The key is that you should not subject the children to your continued hostility. In this case, Pat finally agreed to curb her attendance at the less necessary times and also to discuss this issue with her therapist. Bob accepted the idea that the children enjoyed seeing their mother at these times and that she was not doing this to "take the children away" from him; therefore, he didn't feel like he had to protect his parenting time with the children. He understood that because he had previously approached this with the idea that the children had to make a choice, he had been constantly placing them in a loyalty conflict. You could be sure that if the children somehow reached Mom during these activities, they would not return to Dad. They could not go back and forth freely. In fact, Bob's prohibition had worked in reverse, so that the children tried even harder to get to see Mom. And what tension did this create for the child playing or performing? Thankfully, these parents worked hard to change the situation and the children were freed from experiencing further unnecessary conflict.

The Dance Recital

John and Nancy had been divorced for a few years. They continued to wage the parental war over their only daughter, a nine-year-old. They had filed numerous postdivorce motions and spent thousands upon thousands of dollars on legal fees for their individual attorneys and for the attorney for the minor child. Their daughter was in therapy and so were they. They had been cautioned about the effects of their conflict on their daughter, but to no avail.

Their daughter took dancing lessons and had an annual recital. John planned to attend with his significant other and Nancy planned to attend alone. The recital took place on one of John's parenting days. Therefore, he planned to bring their daughter to the recital and then return with her to his home for the night. John and Nancy hardly spoke to each other and had not discussed the event. They made no advance preparations for their interactions before or after the recital. They instead both discussed the event directly with their daughter. They had their own views of just how the evening would unfold. They were also heavily invested in avoiding contact with the other parent. They had not taken into account the needs and desires of their daughter to have her parents attend the event, act cordially, and allow her access to both of them. At the recital, they did not speak to each other and of course did not sit together. At the end of the recital, John met his daughter and whisked her away before Nancy could even tell her what a good job she had done. Nancy did not get a chance to see, hug, or praise her daughter!

Unfortunately, these parents were so addicted to their conflict that it was very difficult for them to break free from their old behaviors. They were heavily self-focused and could not control their behavior for the sake of their daughter. The best solution here was to set up a very rigid structure for times like these and others. These parents needed lots of rules and could not adapt them to individual situations. It became necessary to define behavioral expectations of these parents in very specific ways. For example, one rule was that each parent will have the chance to see the child for up to five minutes following events and activities so that they could congratulate or console the child and make any appropriate comments about their performance. Both parents agreed to be civil during this exchange and not to make any inappropriate remarks.

The School Concert

Mark and Kate had three children and had been divorced for a number of years. Kate was remarried and Mark was not. The children had some degree of conflict with their new stepfather and objected to their mother's new religious persuasion. Mark had filed for a change of custody, and an attorney for the minor children had been assigned. Protective orders had been filed and the conflict level was significant.

One of the girls had a school concert that both parents planned to attend. Kate was coming with her husband and Mark was coming with his current girlfriend. At times these parents thought that they could be more cooperative than they could actually be. They did not prepare for the event, had very little communication beforehand, and exerted little control over their impulsive, hostile behavior. When Kate and her husband arrived at the concert, Mark was already there with his girlfriend and one of the other siblings. He invited Kate to sit with them and, of course, their daughter was thrilled to be able to sit with both of her parents. Unfortunately, but predictably the conversation turned into an angry exchange sometime during the event. Sarcastic remarks flew and nasty comments were made about Kate's new husband and about Mark's girlfriend. Their daughter witnessed the whole thing.

These parents had to agree to discuss future special events well in advance. They also had to realize that they were not ready to sit together without conflict. They had to agree to sit apart and to follow the parenting rules before and after the event, which would allow them to be face-to-face but not to exchange any conversation other than cordialities. This was unfortunate for their children, who lost the opportunity to see and be with both parents at these special times.

Parents Who Followed the Rules

The Communion Party

Sue and Frank had been divorced for a few years. They had one eight-year-old son. Frank had remarried and had a new baby less than one year of age. Sue had a boyfriend but was not remarried. She also had a chronic illness that sometimes required hospitalization and also required ongoing treatment. When their son completed all the steps to be ready to make his first communion, both sides of the family were excited to share in this event. Sue and Frank had generally been cooperative with one another. However, there were some issues over increasing Frank's parenting time with his son. There were also some issues about Frank making arrangements directly with his son. For example, Frank would often agree to let their son come over or sleep over without first discussing it with Sue. He would make arrangements for activities that he and his son wanted to do together on "Mom's time" without checking it out with Sue prior to making the commitment. This put Sue in a difficult position. How could she say "No" when Frank had already said "Yes"?

Frank and his wife approached Sue about having a joint party for their son after his communion service. They wanted to have the party at their house and said that they would work with Sue on the arrangements. Their son was very excited about everyone getting together for this special time. The next thing Sue knew, she and her family received an invitation to the post-communion party at Frank's home. Sue was extremely upset. She felt left out of the process and now did not want to attend. She then wanted to split the day and have two separate parties. Her biggest concession was to agree to a joint party, but at a neutral place such as a restaurant. A verbal battle, including lots of hurtful remarks and anger, ensued.

When Sue and Frank got together to discuss the problem, it was apparent that Sue was hurt and disappointed. She had trusted Frank and his new wife and so had her family. She believed in cooperative co-parenting and now felt like there had been a major breach. Sue was able to explain her feelings to Frank, who apologized for going forward without her involvement. He thought that she should have made a direct overture offering help, but Sue said she had been waiting to hear from Frank what was needed. Better communication earlier in this process would have eliminated this unfortunate exchange.

In the end, Sue was able to understand the negative impact of changing the arrangements at the last minute. This would be very confusing for their son. Sue accepted Frank's apology and they held the party together as planned—extended family, friends, and all.

The Birthday Party

Rich and Pam, who have three children, have been divorced for several years. Rich is remarried and Pam is not. Pam has a cordial relationship with Rich's new wife. A few weeks before the oldest child was to turn nine, Pam began planning his birthday party at her house. She started inviting a number of the child's friends as well as family members. One evening she and her son were discussing the party, and he lamented the fact that his father would not be there.

Pam proposed the idea that maybe his father *could* be invited. The next day when their son went to visit his father he proposed the idea. The parents didn't get a chance to discuss this beforehand, so it was not clear to Dad that his new wife was not invited. This was their only mistake: They didn't speak to each other first, causing their son to become the messenger and bear some of the parental conflict. These parents worked quickly to resolve the issues and Dad did attend the party alone. His son was overjoyed.

Extended Family

Please remember that extended family members are your responsibility. Their behavior is dependent upon how *you* tell them to act. If they are in the presence of the other parent and/or their extended family, they must be polite and cordial. The children do not need to hear or see their relatives' feelings paraded in front of them. At special events and activities, the focus is supposed to be on the child, and not on others' old hurts and opinions. Your relatives may think that they are somehow supporting you with rude behavior. They think they are being loyal by defending your honor and position. Yet they are misguided. They can do what is best for you by doing what is best for the children. They are present to support their grandchildren, nieces and nephews, etc. If they can't control themselves then they should be told that they will not be invited again. This is your job as parents. You have no right to say that you can't manage your relatives—you can and you must!

Through the Eyes of the Children

At the times of special events and activities, your children should be the center of attention. They are anxious about their performance, excited about your coming to see them, and eager to please their coaches, teachers, and you. Please do not let them down. They should not have to reexperience the old divorce conflicts, especially now. They want so much for everyone to be proud of them, support them, and focus on them. This is not "your" time. It's *their* time. Prepare carefully and structure the situation to maximize a positive interaction. If you truly do not believe that you can behave in front of your children and other family and friends, then attend the event or activity and interact minimally but civilly. Remember that even when your children are performing, they are always watching, listening, and feeling in response to you. They are aware of what you do and say. Give them what they truly need from you.

CHAPTER 10

New Relationships, Old Issues

Moving On

Parents have every right to go on with their lives after divorce. The expectation is that there will be new relationships, which hopefully will provide new love, caring, and understanding for the parent and his/her children. Many parents assume that their children will also accept and appreciate new significant others just because they feel that way themselves. Other parents feel that it is their turn to be happy too, and the children will just have to adjust. Some parents cannot tolerate the loneliness and look to include others in their parenting time to help with the children and to take away some of the feelings that being a single parent generates. These assumptions and expectations stem from the parent's needs and not always those of the children. Many children will spend some of their childhood years in stepfamily relationships. Other children will live with their parents' new partners outside of a marriage. There are new roles for everyone, and parents need to handle the introduction of new relationships and potential or committed stepparents thoughtfully and sensitively. Although each family situation is unique, there are some general issues that should be addressed.

The Children's Fantasies

Parents like to assume that children of divorce are relieved to see the fighting end, but that is not actually what the children may be thinking. Most children work hard to deny the possibility of their parents' divorce, even during the highest level of the parents' marital conflict. They wish that their parents would work things out, and they often try to help that process by injecting themselves into the fray. They work as peacemakers, parentified children, substitute spouses, caretakers, etc. Even when this effort on their part does not work out and a divorce occurs, children often maintain their fantasies for many years to come. They continue to fantasize about the possible reconciliation of their parents.

These reconciliation fantasies interfere with the children's ability to form close relationships with new stepparents. In high-conflict families, these fantasies are sometimes even stronger and more entrenched because of the very nature of the parents' continued hostile involvement and interactions. High-conflict parents are often still significantly connected to each other. Their fighting keeps them in contact, attorney letters arrive often, messages are left frequently, e-mails abound, many days continue to be spent in court, and large amounts of money are spent on the process. When parents learn to co-parent in a cooperative and businesslike manner, children can begin to let go of their reconciliation fantasies. At the same time, they can start to go on with their own lives instead of playing the role of marriage counselor or mediator. They are then free to integrate their parents' new relationships into their lives without the burden of feeling disloyal to one parent or the other.

Dating: A Brave New World

Divorced parents begin to date for many reasons. Those who got involved in relationships prior to the legal end of their marriage are quick to continue that involvement and are often ready for these relationships to go forward faster than their children and certainly their ex-spouses can tolerate. Others are just lonely and need the companionship of others and the acknowledgement that they are still interesting and attractive. Some are scared of being alone. These parents may rush into relationships too soon just to fill the void left by the dissolution of their marriage. Some experience newfound freedom and begin to relive the years that may have been dedicated to marriage and children when they should have, in part, been dedicated to establishing their own individuality and individuation from their own parents. Finally, some are ready to begin their new lives and explore new relationships with much forethought and consideration of the needs of their children and the impact of new relationships on their new family unit.

When parents are ready to date, children are not always ready. In fact, sometimes it seems children will never be ready! There are many child-related issues that accompany your decision to engage in new relationships.

The End of the Reunification Fantasy

This was discussed in the above section. Keep in mind that it's a primary concern of your children.

Fear of Abandonment

Children of divorce are always coping with the loss of their parents' marriage. Sometimes this also includes the loss of their old home, friends, school, pets, etc. They are sensitized to the possibility of loss and even expect relationships to be unstable. Their world has changed dramatically. In high-conflict families, children experience this at a more intense level. The conflict level may force parents to communicate infrequently or not at all. If the parent introduces new relationships, the children naturally worry and wonder if these people who offer them the hope of a happy new family may leave them as well. This shapes the level at which they are willing to invest in their parents' new friends.

Not surprisingly, children also worry that if you have someone else in your life, you will abandon them. They may think, "If [first parent] stopped loving [second parent], how do I know they won't stop loving me, now that they have their new friend?"

Too Many Adjustments

Children of divorce must contend with multiple changes in relationships with their parents, siblings, and extended family. When

new relationships are introduced too soon, children can find it difficult to solidify their connections with their parents as new family
units. Instead of seeing their parent as capable of caring for them,
they are forced to go through their parents' relationships and
self-exploration along with them. This is one more adjustment that
they just do not need. It interferes with the parent and child roles and
exposes children to adult dilemmas and emotions. Not only is it
unnecessary, it overwhelms children with situations for which they
have not developed mature coping mechanisms. High-conflict parents are more likely not to recognize that their children are being
bombarded by all the changes the divorce asks them to make. These
parents are much too busy taking care of their own needs and protecting themselves against the real and imagined assaults of their
ex-spouse.

Loyalty Issues

Children of divorce are torn between the need to inform one
parent of the introduction of new relationships and the desire to protect the other parent's privacy and that of their new family unit.
Especially in high-conflict situations, the children expect the parent to
react negatively when there is the mere mention of anyone new in
the life of the other parent. Sometimes they keep this secret and,
sadly, sometimes they are even told by one parent to do so. "You
don't want to upset Mom, so let's not tell her that we went for pizza
with Sue." At other times they excitedly discuss their weekend, only
to find out that they have made mom or dad feel sad or angry. They
may have even caused more conflict between their warring parents!
At the same time, they want to please the other parent by "liking"
their new friend. They may not be sure of how they feel. Instead,
their feelings are at the mercy of their conflicting parents' emotions.
They go back and forth trying to please both parents—or they may
choose sides and set out to destroy or defend their parent's new
relationship.

Conducting Your New Relationship

The most important tenet to remember is that your children do not
need to be involved in your new relationship until there is a serious
commitment. This generally means that you can date all you want on
your own time, but you shouldn't introduce the children to your new

partners until you are as certain as possible that this relationship is headed in a very serious direction. This helps to minimize the potential that the children will experience another loss. Children of divorce often have a tenuous view of relationships, and it's not healthy to reinforce that perception by exposing them to repetitions of the loss they experience through divorce. Children can quickly become quite attached to these new people and may not understand when you have to tell them that he or she will not be coming over for dinner ever again.

In addition, your children need your attention. If your attention is diverted by your new relationship or your busy dating life, your children may not be getting what they need from you. Divorce requires significant recuperation time, and introducing children to new people who they may perceive will take you away from them will not necessarily facilitate your children's adaptation. If these new people have children themselves, then the situation becomes even more complicated. And they may worry that you will like those children more than you like them. Your children may not want to share you just yet! Your children may not want to share their home with others, especially if they are just getting used to it themselves. You may find your involvement in relationships with others helpful, but your children may not. Listen to their needs.

It is vital that divorced parents spend time first forming their own new family unit before throwing new individuals into this mixture. You need to spend time together—just the two, three, or four of you. You need to live together, cook together, decorate together, play together, and vacation together. You need to cry together, talk together, laugh together, learn together, and heal together. Introducing new people just helps to avoid this process or perhaps move it along too rapidly. Children then get the idea that they are expected to move forward quickly and get over the divorce on *your* time schedule. Even if *you* want to avoid dealing with all your feelings after the divorce, please do not impose this on your children.

One advantage of having a parenting plan is that you have time off from the children. You know in advance when this will take place and can plan accordingly. That means you don't need to date during your time with the children. They should be your only priority during their time with you. Separate these two areas of your life and give them both the attention that they deserve.

In high-conflict cases, this principle is even more imperative. Parents are often still raw and find new relationships supportive and reinforcing to their tattered self-esteem. They may also be confused by their feelings toward their ex-spouse and use new relationships to be vindictive. They are often more concerned about getting back at the other parent by imposing new relationships upon the children. They secretly hope that the children will tell the other parent about this person and their great Sunday afternoon. That will *surely* get a reaction!

Here are some guidelines for conducting new relationships in a healthy manner that takes the children's feelings into consideration.

New relationships should be conducted in privacy. Use your nonparenting time.

Only introduce new relationships when they have become committed. The children should be protected from the potential of experiencing another significant loss.

Tell the children about new relationships in a clear and thoughtful manner. Select a time when you can talk with them and answer their questions. Anticipate their questions and feelings. Reassure them that you will keep them fully informed about the extent of your feelings for one another and your future plans. Be clear that the relationship does not diminish your love for your children. You have plenty of love to go around.

Keep your initial meetings involving the children structured and short. Plan to do things together for specific periods of time. These should not be open-ended and should not extend beyond the stated time frame, even if you are having a great time.

Establish appropriate limits with your new partner. You may need to define the role of your new partner for the partner. Tell them exactly what you have told the children and what to expect from the children. Help them to understand the possible range of the children's emotions.

Do not involve your new partner every time you see the children. The children need time to adapt, and they still need time with you alone.

Inform the other parent before you tell the children. This is the right and decent thing to do. More importantly, it absolves the children from being placed in loyalty conflicts. They will often ask if the other parent knows. They don't want to be the messengers of this news nor should they be expected to do your work for you. They should not have to experience the other parent's initial reaction, and they should not get caught up in any potential conflict between the two of you.

Reacting to Your Ex's New Relationship

Yes, you need to be civilized about your ex-spouse's new relationship. You may not yet be able to process your anger and hurt in an appropriate manner. You may be highly reactive to new persons in the life of your ex and have great difficulty controlling your responses. Nevertheless, you have an obligation to your children to do just that. And so does your ex-spouse when it comes to *your* new partner. The tendency here is to take this ideal opportunity to communicate your dissatisfaction to the children through nonverbal cues, sarcasm, avoidance, or even angry words. The children are then put in a position where they must make choices between their parents. If they like the new partner then they will displease and be disloyal to one parent, and if they reject the person they will displease or be disloyal to the other. The children remain stuck with you in the divorce and cannot go on with their new lives. You may want to remain there, but you don't have to keep your children addicted to the conflict along with you.

Children's Reactions to New Relationships

Children of divorce have a wide range of reactions when they meet their parents' new significant others. These can range from very negative to highly positive. Your children are often less predictable than you think, so don't underestimate them. You certainly can hope that the children will be accepting of your new relationship, but realize that this won't always be the case. Children in high-conflict situations are usually the most confused because they assume that this person will ignite more flames between their parents. They expect negative reactions.

The range of the children's reactions may be:

Passive acceptance—These children do not express their feelings directly; they are calm on the surface and quietly go along with the new relationship.

Overt anger and aggression—These children refuse to see the new significant other and sometimes the parent too. They may also act out in destructive or self-destructive ways and can make the situation very difficult and awkward.

Passive aggressive behavior—These children engage in activities in which they seek to undermine the parent's relationship with the other person, while on the surface they are compliant.

Genuine acceptance—These children have been prepared well, have had time with the other parent, and feel that they have a voice in the situation. They begin to develop a relationship with the new significant other.

Protection of the other parent—These children may reject the new person just because they feel that they must act out the other parent's wishes. They are caught up in loyalty issues and act as agents of the hurt or angry parent.

Keeping secrets—These children may be trying to adapt to a new person in the life of one parent, but they will keep those interactions a secret from the other parent. They try not to get involved in their parents' conflict and do not want to be messengers. This places an enormous burden on children who naturally want to share their experiences with those they love.

The best way by which you can assess your child's reaction is to process these visits afterward. Sit down and talk with them so you can clarify any misperceptions. Give them permission to talk with the other parent about their experiences. Tell them that they have complete freedom to discuss anything with the other parent. (You should have already prepared the other parent for this feedback.) Dispel the myth that keeping secrets is helpful. Take them out of the role of go-between.

High-conflict parents tend to avoid discussing their new relationships. They expect the other parent to react negatively. The other parent often assumes that this new relationship is designed to hurt them all over again. They feel jealous and reexperience old issues. It feels easier to just not talk about it at all. This leaves the other parent in the dark, often making them think they have no choice but to get their information by questioning the children. You can choose the inevitable road of conflict by withholding information or being secretive or provocative about new relationships. You can choose the road of cooperative co-parenting by being informative and preparing all involved, including your ex-spouse.

When New Relationships Are Old Issues

The most difficult situation is when a new significant other has been (or is suspected to have been) involved with one parent before the marriage ended. It is also hard when this type of relationship begins very soon after the divorce, leaving little time for everyone to adjust to the new situation. It is in the best interests of the children that the parent not pursue this relationship in any overt manner. Parents can't be prevented from going forth to live their own lives, but they do need to take into consideration the effect on their children. Children need an opportunity to build their new family units. They may have to adjust to moves and other new surroundings. A new relationship can cause them to feel an even greater sense of loss than the divorce has already imposed. They will miss their parent, whose time and energy is now shared. Unfortunately, the children's feelings may get completely lost in the midst of the comfort and excitement that their parent is experiencing. Parents *must* ask themselves whose needs they are serving by pursuing these relationships without respect for the feelings of the children.

Parents should also be careful about immediately accepting the children's overt reactions. Children in the early stages after divorce are focused on pleasing both parents. If that means that one parent wants them to like a new significant other and maybe his or her family, then they may do so just to please their parent. They most certainly do not want to lose the affection. They cannot tolerate another loss, and they worry that if they object, the parent might just not love them anymore. Therefore, sometimes children will act the part, verbalize their agreement, and not express any negative feelings about the situation when they really do have some strong concerns.

Another issue here is the reaction of the other parent. As you can imagine, this type of situation will just fuel the flame of conflict. It is very hard for a parent in a high-conflict divorce situation to be concerned about the other parent's feelings, but perhaps they can understand that increasing conflict by outwardly engaging in this type of relationship too soon will create an untenable, hostile environment for their children. The other parent is likely to feel even more abandoned, rejected, and disrespected. They may have a harder time parenting at all, let alone parenting cooperatively. This can spill over to the children in terms of what is said to them, what is communicated through them, and where the focus resides during this critical phase just before and after divorce. Again, you have choices as parents, and you can avoid exacerbating conflict by making decisions that will protect your children. Keep your relationships to yourselves and introduce them properly and at the best time possible.

Lastly, as parents you are the moral examples for your children. Your behavior will come back to haunt you in their adolescence and beyond. They take their cues from you and watch your every move. You will need to be able to give them appropriate explanations for your decisions. You will need to be able to set limits on their requests about the boundaries of relationships and reconcile those with your own behavior. Younger children have difficulty with discrepancies because they think in very black-and-white, rule-oriented terms. Older children will challenge you and expect to be treated in the same way that you treat yourself and others. It will be harder to say "No" if you are doing it yourself. "Do as I say and not as I do" won't hold much weight with your adolescents.

Remarriage

Remarriage for one or both parents in high-conflict families is a very tender process. It can stimulate many old issues and recreate many of the predivorce and early postdivorce feelings. Ex-spouses again feel hurt and rejected. There are some common, overt concerns:

- What will be the place of the biological child in the new family unit?

- How will this affect the financial situation?

- How much time will the parent now spend with the biological child?

- What will the living arrangements be now? Will rooms be shared, etc.?

- Is the stepparent an "acceptable" parent?

- How do the stepparent and ex-spouse get along?

- How do the stepparent and his or her ex-spouse get along?

- How much will the stepparent and ex-spouse actually have to interact?

- How should those interactions be conducted?

- What is the role of the stepparent in the life of the children? How involved do they get in direct day-to-day care? How involved do they get in decision making and discipline?

- What is the quality of the parent and stepparent marriage? What is their lifestyle? What are their moral standards?

- Are the parent and stepparent planning on having more children?

- Do my children have to deal with and maybe even live with the stepparent's children?

These are very difficult questions to answer in even the very lowest-conflict divorce cases. In high-conflict cases, these answers can become impossible to find without extreme hostility. Remarriage provides a whole new breeding ground for trouble. Children anticipate and experience anger and hurt, whether it's underlying or overt. This makes their own adjustment to the new situation harder and more confusing. Here they can especially feel like they are spies, carrying information back and forth from one side to the other.

The answers to the above questions are really unique to each new stepfamily, but there are some overall suggestions that can help to minimize the conflict in even the most hostile cases. Ideally, of course, it's best if both parents and stepparent can work together in the best interests of the children. There are some wonderful stepparents who are capable of balancing their own needs in the new marriage with those of their new spouse, new stepchildren, and even their own biological children. In remarriage the responsibility level grows exponentially, and one has to have the capability and willingness to take the perspective of all others involved.

Generally, the minimum expected in the relationship between a stepparent and the other biological parent is civility, cordiality, decency, and a basic level of appropriate interaction. Sometimes this is also the maximum that can be expected from high-conflict parents. Their hostility level rises to such a significant level that they have difficulty interacting at all when the new spouse is present. Children need all their parents (adoptive, biological, *and* stepparents) to act like adults and create an environment that will allow their lives to go forward. If stepparent and ex-spouse conflict interferes to the point that children's schedules, events, school information, and social lives become compromised, the children can suffer enormous consequences. These areas become the battleground for all the old issues that have resurfaced with the new marriage and stepfamily. Of course, it would surely be ideal if all parents could not only get along but also interact nicely and exchange pleasantries around the children. Many parents who try hard to go forth with their lives and help their children to do the same are able to accomplish this awesome task. They reap the rewards of seeing their children released from loyalty concerns and the anticipatory anxiety that can accompany parent-stepparent interactions.

High-conflict parents choose secretiveness over full disclosure. They tend not to tell the other parent all the information they request about the new spouse and family. While privacy is certainly important to the new family, the other parent also has some vested interest in this person who has come to live with and take care of their children. A lack of disclosure will only exacerbate the situation. The children literally may not know what to do. They could want to share their weekends with the other parent but feel like they just might be the cause of a war. They may even make things worse by revealing things that one parent does not want shared. They do not know how to please both parents at the same time. They are truly caught in the middle—alone with their own feelings—and are simultaneously focused on caring for the feelings of both of their parents.

Stepparents vary in the level of involvement in and parenting of their spouse's children from other marriages. Some are highly active parents, caring for these children on a daily basis, whereas others have more of a friendship, perhaps with some parental responsibilities. The question always arises as to whether or not stepparents should have a voice in the co-parenting between the divorced parents. In our program we do not automatically invite the stepparents into sessions. We do ask them to come into meetings when there is any conflict between the stepparent and the new spouse. They never attend all the parent meetings. The purpose here is to underscore and strengthen the relationship between the biological parents. They are the primary decision makers who need to learn to work together. The stepparent offers his/her opinion through their spouse. We work to restructure the relationship between the parents but are most interested in quelling the conflict for the sake of the children. Some stepparents resent this approach, but in most cases it allows the parents to work on their own parenting issues without interference, except perhaps behind the scenes.

Similarly, parents need to allow for the differences that may occur in both new homes. When one stepfamily is composed of five children and the other family of one or two, schedules, rules, and other structures may be quite different. Ideally, the homes should be as consistent as possible. Yet, these are two unique cultures that may have very disparate needs. You cannot parent over the others' doorstep, so you will need to allow for variations. In one home a child may be allowed to prepare a separate meal when they do not care for what is being served for dinner. In a family of seven this would cause chaos and is not acceptable. The rule there is that you eat what is cooked. The children may not like these differences and may use them to manipulate their parents, but they must adhere to what is expected in each home. Be sensitive to the position in which this places the children. The level of adaptation required is hard for them, especially the younger ones. Help them to adjust to the differences instead of making it harder by asserting your way as the best and only way. There is more than one road that will lead to the destination.

New Relationships and a New Future

When a divorce occurs, parents should seek to grieve the loss of the marriage and to successfully go on with their lives and those of their children. Part of that process may include new relationships and/or new spouses. They hope that their children will have positive feelings toward these people. They hope that their new relationships will create opportunities for the children to form a new and complete family unit that may even include new siblings. If you form such a relationship, it is easy to forget how complicated this may become for your ex-spouse and the children. They aren't always as ready to go on with your life as you are. New relationships may spark old issues as well as new concerns. Pay attention to your children's feelings and, yes, pay attention to the feelings of your ex-spouse. They too affect the children's attitude and adjustment. If you engage your children, new spouse and family, and ex-spouse in a cooperative manner, then your children will have the chance to experience a more caring, nurturing, loving, and lasting committed relationship. This is going to be your future and theirs. The two are intricately connected.

CHAPTER 11

Parent Alienation

What Is Parent Alienation?

Definition

The concept of parent alienation has been defined in varying ways by
different authors in this field. Wallerstein and Kelly (1980) described
children who are torn by their anger for one parent versus the other.
They become the ally of one parent and turn against the other parent,
sometimes even prior to the marital separation and certainly beyond.
Gardner (1998) really first coined the term parent alienation syndrome (PAS) to include, "A disturbance in which children are preoccupied with deprecation and criticism of a parent—denigration that
is unjustified and/or exaggerated" (73). He goes on to say that parent
alienation includes "not only conscious and unconscious factors
within the preferred parent that contribute to the parent's influencing
the child's alienation. Furthermore, it includes factors that arise
within the child ... that foster the development of this syndrome"
(73). Although Dr. Gardner believes that in parent alienation syndrome criticism of the other parent must be exaggerated and/or
unjustified, other authors do not think that this is always the case.
Douglas Darnall (1998) states that "One parent can alienate the children against the other simply by harping on faults that are real and

provable" (5). He goes on to say, "You can't assume that the targeted parent is without fault. Targeted parents can also become alienators when they retaliate because of their hurt. This puts them in the role of the alienator while the other parent becomes the victim. The roles become blurred because it's difficult to know who is the alienator and who is the targeted parent. Often both parents feel victimized. It is important to remember that alienation is a process, not a person" (5).

Before and after a divorce, or even if parents were never married, it is essential that children be encouraged to love both individuals. Alienation can have immediate and long-lasting effects on children, contributing to difficulties in forming relationships well into adulthood. Unfortunately, conflict and litigation are heavy contributors to the formation of parent alienation syndrome. Custody evaluations and court battles serve to set up alignments and place family members in opposing camps. Parents can hardly help prevent the competition from starting as they try to portray themselves in a better light than the other parent. Even parents who are well-meaning and try to have their children's best interests at heart can find themselves caught up in the struggle. Tone of voice, nonverbal cues, insinuating remarks, and minor interference with the parenting plan schedule can all establish the roots of parent alienation. Avoidance of this behavior requires a lifelong, conscious effort to monitor your behavior and that of your children. High-conflict divorces that are particularly adversarial in nature are ripe for PAS to develop. Unfortunately, with high-conflict parents the situations are well beyond early prevention and often far along the road to parent alienation.

Identification

Parent alienation syndrome is usually identified by observing the behavior of the parents and their relationship with the children. There are certain behaviors that seem to characterize the alienating parent and similar behaviors that characterize the alienated child. These may include:

Alienating Parent

- Believes that the child does not need to be parented by the other parent

- Allows the child to make independent decisions related to the parenting plan schedule

- Depicts the other parent as dangerous and not healthy for the child

- Makes denigrating remarks about the other parent

- Exaggerates the weaknesses of the other parent

- Hinders face-to-face and/or phone contact by interfering with the schedule and creating obstacles to phone calls or other communication

- Makes excessive contact with the child when child is staying with the other parent

- Involves the child in discussing adult issues such as the causes for the divorce, divorce agreements, and finances

- Interrogates the child after child stays with the other parent

- Encourages the child's criticisms of the other parent and sympathizes with the child's negative viewpoint

Alienated Child

- Openly expresses hatred and dislike of the targeted parent

- Presents unrealistic, exaggerated reasons

- Refuses to speak to or visit the targeted parent

- Shows little or no evidence of guilt or upset over behavior

- Gives reasons that are seemingly rehearsed and repetitious

- Evidences extremely upsetting behavior if forced to visit or talk with targeted parent

- Allies with the alienating parent to the point where the child repeats the words of that parent, mimicking their thoughts and arguments

- Has access to and repeats inappropriate information that should only be available to adults

- Plays the role of spy for the alienating parent

- The child describes things in a very restricted and black and white manner, thus creating a schism between the parents.

For high-conflict parents, it is very difficult to sort out whether there is clear evidence of parent alienation. The battling is so intense that children sometimes cannot help but interfere with the parenting plan by refusing to visit or take phone calls or e-mail from the other parent. They want so much for the war to stop that they will join any force that may seem to make that promise possible. Children caught in the middle are potentially at risk for any number of symptoms. Generally, it is believed that the long-term impact on children and families who are experiencing parent alienation can be quite severe. They may be likely to develop a range of pathological behaviors, including:

- Difficulty in forming intimate relationships, especially later in life

- Difficulty in managing anger and hostility in their relationships

- Conflicts with others, especially with persons in positions of authority

- Psychosomatic symptoms, including anxiety and depression manifested by disturbances in sleeping and eating, energy level, interest level, and even by suicidal ideation

- An inability to move forward with their lives due to the obsession with the target parent

The effects of parent alienation are rarely mild. They are dangerous and often very severe. The degree of severity will depend upon how long the alienation has been going on and how firmly the alienation attempts have taken hold. In addition, the age of the child, the support network, the child's previous relationship with the targeted parent, and the child's degree of enmeshment with the alienating parent all play major roles in determining the extent of the syndrome and the effectiveness of the intervention techniques.

Reasons for Parent Alienation Syndrome

There are many reasons why parents get caught in the traps that lead to parent alienation syndrome. The difficulties of divorce naturally evolve into battles that cause friends and family members to take their places in support of one parent or the other. As we have stated previously, this is the worst scenario for the children. They want to be able to negotiate the changes in their lives, but they cannot do this if they need to protect one parent against the other. Parents whose own psychological boundaries are poor become enmeshed with their children and cannot keep their own issues separate. Some common reasons for allowing or even encouraging PAS to develop are:

Guilt

Parents feel guilty after a divorce. They experience the sadness and anger displayed by their children. They then often try to become the super mom or dad of the century. The only way to do this is by putting down the other parent.

Blame

Many parents have not yet come to terms with the reasons for their divorce. They feel the need to blame the other parent. By doing so they set the stage for alienating the children. Blaming is very powerful, and in cases of PAS it can even be likened to brainwashing. Children feel that they have no choice but to join with the angry, blaming parent.

Parent-in-Charge Status

In many families, one parent has been the "parent in charge" during most of the lives of the children. When a divorce occurs and joint custody is awarded and/or a shared parenting plan is established, the other parent has newfound decision-making authority and caretaking responsibilities. The "parent in charge" resents having to consult and actively co-parent with the other. Why should they have to discuss whether or not the children should be enrolled in soccer? They always made that decision themselves in the past! Welcome to the world of divorce and joint decision making. Two parents now must make these choices together. This is especially true for unmarried parents who have not had any significant history together as parents. One parent (usually the mother) wants to hold the reins tightly and treat the other parent as a visitor in the life of the child. "Parent-in-charge" status often leads to the possibility of PAS because the perception of the other parent is that he or she is not "good enough," not experienced enough, and given past history has not earned their status as an equal parent.

Sexist Attitudes

Stereotypes still abound and contribute to the notion that fathers are not as capable of caring for their children as mothers. This is most often true in the case of younger children and female children. Fathers are thought to be the "baby-sitters" instead of the responsible parent. Attitudes have been changing since the 1980s, but there is still a long way to go. Fathers have been successfully pursuing their right to be actively involved in their children's lives and the courts have started to recognize these issues.

Protection

In some cases of PAS, a parent feels that they have to protect the children from potential abuse by the other parent. Sometimes a spouse has been abused physically and/or verbally during the marriage and is concerned that their children are potentially in danger when with the other parent. In other cases one parent is concerned that the other parent has a substance abuse problem or a mental illness that would put the children at risk. When these situations are accurate and serious, the children need and should be *appropriately* protected from the other parent. Unfortunately, parents will use these issues and especially their own past marital history to accuse the other parent. These kinds of accusations will usually result in the involvement of police, family relations officers, lawyers, custody evaluators, and the courts. The basis for the highest levels of conflict is then established. In addition, children are often restricted from seeing the other parent while the "truth" is being determined—and thus begins the process of PAS. The children get used to not seeing the other parent regularly and may believe that they need protection.

Fears and Loneliness

Adjusting to being alone as a single parent and a single person is difficult. Sometimes parents subtly teach children that they need to fill the void left by the end of the marriage. They tell the children how much they missed them and how lonely they feel when the children are with the other parent. They themselves fear the emptiness and convey that to their children. The children naturally stay close at hand to assuage those painful feelings for their parent, and they may blame the other parent for causing the pain in the first place.

Intense Anger

The roots of PAS often grow from the extraordinary anger that one parent experiences toward the other parent. They may have felt deceived, wronged, or taken advantage of—but whatever the issue, they want revenge. After the divorce, the only vehicle through which a parent can continue to express these feelings is the children. If the parent can get the children on his or her side, the anger can flow through them in a way that will be most hurtful to the other parent. The co-parenting relationship becomes the only means to shoot psychological poison darts at the ex-spouse. The children are then the messengers of one parent's venom.

Case Studies

There are many gradations of PAS, exemplified by numerous cases. Below we outline two such examples.

The Good Divorce

Linda and Dan were married for about fifteen years before their divorce. They had two children: Liz, age ten, and Josh, age thirteen. The divorce was mutually agreed to and presented by both parents to the children. Dan and Linda remember that Liz left the room very upset upon hearing that her parents were parting. The parents went about setting up an ideal situation for co-parenting. The family home was to be sold and both parents were to purchase homes within the same school district and very near one another. Dan worked full-time and Linda was a stay-at-home mother. There was enough alimony and child support for Linda to continue to stay home and care for the children. The parenting plan called for the children to go back and forth between the homes on an almost fifty/fifty basis. These parents even planned to continue to share a summer cottage to which they would each take the children for consecutive vacation weeks.

Dan hadn't had as much of a "hands on" relationship in the day-to-day caretaking of the children when they were young, but he now wanted to have the children come home from school to his house and to see them and live with them on a regular basis. Linda agreed to this plan at the time of the divorce but came from a background where at-home mothering was the norm. In addition, even though the divorce was relatively amicable, the events leading up to this decision created some degree of hurt, distrust, and anger.

Josh adjusted to the divorce beautifully. He enjoyed both of his parents and developed an excellent relationship with each of them. He not only followed the parenting plan but also went back and forth freely according to his own needs. Liz resisted the plan from the start. She would go over to her dad's house but not really follow the schedule. She would find reasons to go over to Mom's after school before going to Dad's and often Mom would pick her up from school as well. She and Mom would make some plans to do a few things after school on days that she should be at Dad's. They reasoned that, after all, he wasn't going to be home for a few hours. Eventually, after about one year, Liz didn't want to go over to Dan's on the pre-determined weekday schedule and started finding reasons to return to Linda's at various times over the weekends. More importantly, she voiced strong negative feelings about being with her father. She was overtly rude and made statements about and to him that most parents would not tolerate. There was no history of abuse or neglect or any trauma between Liz and her father. Yet the time with her father continued to decrease to the point where Liz would only see her father if absolutely necessary. Interestingly enough, she would visit with him and her brother and sometimes extended family if an event was planned. She adjusted at these times but would not stay over if there were no specific plans.

The family saw a number of professionals who all recommended that Liz be required to keep to the original parenting plan. Linda claimed that she could not force Liz to go and then began to voice that she believed that Liz should have a significant voice in designing her own plan. Finally, upon recommendation of Dan's lawyer, Linda and Dan entered the P.E.A.C.E. Program. The intervention included meetings with both parents for well over a year. It also included meetings with Liz, individual therapy for Liz, and family therapy for Liz and her father, Liz and her mother, and sometimes Liz and both of her parents. Recommendations were offered, but Linda had difficulty enforcing them. She was told not to take care of Liz during the time that she was supposed to be with her father. In fact, it was recommended that she go away for a weekend or not be home some of those evenings. Linda did not really comply, and Liz got worse. In therapy it was clear that there was really nothing substantially wrong between Liz and her father. Her anger was very exaggerated and she was waging a campaign that had no basis in reality. Dan persevered, endured, and continued to attend games, invite Liz over, and call her. He had a hard time not expressing some anger and exasperation, but kept trying. He tried to set limits on her verbal abuse, which just made her even more rejecting.

The message was subtle but clear. Linda did not believe that Liz should have to keep to the parenting plan, and Linda quietly and indirectly reinforced Liz's behavior by not establishing that it was absolutely in her best interests to see her father. PAS encroached like a slow-growing cancer and ravaged this good divorce. In this case a return to court was determined to be necessary and seemed to be the only recourse. The court was limited in what motions could be filed so a custody evaluation was ordered. Dan didn't really want custody—he just wanted Liz to be with him when she should. Linda knew this, but the court had to be involved to give Linda the backbone and support to enforce the parenting plan. This is a very sad situation that didn't have to end up with such a high conflict level. No one wanted to return to court—including the attorneys—but the court's voice, structure, and power became imperative to decrease the PAS and its impact.

Mom and Her Girls

Cara and Jim were married for thirteen years. They had three girls, ages twelve, ten, and seven. Their divorce agreement did not specify any particular parenting plan, and just ten months after the divorce they returned to court. The girls were not staying over at their father's home and he felt that Cara was trying to alienate them. The girls voiced their support of their mother and denigrated their father and his fiancé. Jim's lawyer filed a contempt of court motion. A guardian *ad litem* was appointed and the battle began in earnest. A very wise judge was asked to rule on this case and this is what he said:

> *"During the marriage, Mr., you were not as involved with your family or children as you should have been. Some of that is attributable to your work schedule, and although you and Mrs. and the children benefited from whatever benefits came out of the work schedule it might have been a mistake. Some of it is also attributable to your pursuit of your own outside interests as the marriage was going along. And that is unfortunate because that is, in part, responsible for what has occurred since then. You caused resentment on the part of your wife and you deserved resentment from your wife. But*

whatever happened until the date that you people got divorced, it does not—it is not sufficient to cause you to be exiled from your children's lives nor is it sufficient to cause them to be exiled from your life. . . . Ms., this has to do with you. You're playing it like a trump. You're building a history around it that is, in effect, building a future. It is the Court's opinion that it is in the best interest of the children to have as much involvement in the life of their father as is possible . . . Since the divorce, Ms., I believe that you have systematically and consistently deprived the children of their opportunity to have a relationship with their father, in violation of these orders. That you have systematically and consistently undermined the feelings of affection and respect that they should have for their father . . . In addition to that, I find that you have covertly worked to undermine the girls' confidence in their ability to have a relationship with their father and to some extent with other people. You've let them know that you depend upon them as allies and as companions . . .

The first result of this is that the kids are being positioned to take care of you. The second result of this is the kids are being positioned to learn how to manipulate people, that there is a reward for manipulating people and that if they don't like their father it's going to be better for you . . . All of my findings and orders are based upon what I believe to be in the best interest of the children . . ."

The judge in this case ordered that: 1) The mother would pay the father's attorney's fees. 2) The mother would pay the fees of the guardian *ad litem* to date. 3) A $10,000 bond was to be posted by the mother as security for any additional costs that might arise if there was any further noncompliance. 4) Both mother and father were to foster respect for the other parent and any other significant others and extended family. The guardian ad litem requested that 5) The children remain in individual/sibling therapy and 6) The parents enter the P.E.A.C.E. Program. To date the parenting plan is in place. The girls are complying. The parents still differ in their parenting styles but are trying to work together. They attend the P.E.A.C.E. Program on a monthly basis. All lawyers have been dismissed at their own request and at that of the parents, except for the mother's attorney. This was truly a positive move toward calming the parent conflict.

Remedies for Parent Alienation Syndrome

The courts have yet to be clear about the preferred choices for judgments of PAS. Most agree that quick judicial intervention that allocates compensatory and consistent time with the child for the alienated parent is in order. In addition, they usually appoint a parent counselor and/or require parent education to facilitate increased understanding of the seriously detrimental effects of parent alienation on children. Many times the children and the parents are all ordered into therapy. Generally, the court moves to provide clear direction and structure to the family. The court order needs to be very specific as to times and dates and conditions of the parenting plan. It usually will direct everyone to comply with the order and outlines potential sanctions for noncompliance.

In the more serious cases where the child or children are strongly enmeshed with the alienating parent, there is a range of possible solutions offered. The least severe is the appointment of a parent coordinator (Garrity and Baris 1994) who takes responsibility for monitoring the compliance with the court order. They have authority to report to the court and require compliance if one parent is not cooperating. The most extreme position is taken by Gardner (1998). He recommends a change of custody away from the alienating parent or from joint custody to the alienated parent. This can sometimes entail little to no initial contact with the alienating parent for a set period of time.

Guidelines for Preventing Parent Alienation Syndrome

As we've described, high-conflict parents are more prone to the possibility of PAS. The battling lends itself to interference with the parenting plan and opportunities for revenge. The hurt and anger is so intense that it is easy to fall into the position of encouraging negative views of the other parent and even articulating them. The hate and distrust that one parent may have felt toward the other parent about the ending of the marriage is easily translated into the children's interactions. The children become the parent's mouthpiece and verbalize the hostility for them. Sometimes these children become unrecognizable. They are so bonded to the alienating parent that they lose the ability to make their own judgments. Their negative remarks and the way they act out at the alienated parent seem planned and repetitive. Children need the chance to separate their feelings from those of their parent, think for themselves, formulate their own opinions, and act independently. They need to be able to form their own relationship with the alienated parent without interference and without having to feel like they are betraying the alienating parent. These children truly bear the burden of divorce in its worst form. There is some thought that when these children get older, they will be able to reattach to the alienated parent as an adult, free of the obligations to the alienating parent that plagued their childhood. There is not enough research available yet to predict whether or not this is true. So let's not take that chance. Let's give children the permission to love both of their parents and to be free to develop those relationships without carrying their parents' old divorce issues forward for them into the postdivorce parenting relationship.

The following are some guidelines for parents who are willing to recognize that PAS is a possibility for them and their children and who want to prevent it. Often this recognition comes from listening to a therapist and/or attorneys. Listen carefully because your children may carry lifelong scars if they are victims of a parentectomy.

Do not interfere with the parenting plan. Your parenting plan was developed to give some organization to the co-parenting schedule and to allow the children time with both of their parents. Obviously, deviations from the plan that allow the children to redesign the schedule or not to go at all fly in the face of this goal. They also give the children a message that the other parent is not important, equal, or even necessary. Once this process begins, it is hard to change. Children will take their cues from the alienating parent and change the plan to meet that parent's needs.

Do not say derogatory things about the other parent. This is a rule that has already been emphasized in this book. Yet it is so vitally important that it bears repeating over and over again. Children of high-conflict divorce have heard enough. They need to form their own relationships with each parent and not be influenced by your views. It is extremely hurtful to the children for one parent to demean the other parent.

Do not expose the children to divorce material meant for adults only. Please remember that these are children and not your adult friends. They need their movies screened, their CDs rated, and their TV monitored. They should not have access to your divorce papers, subsequent legal actions, custody reports, etc. Protect them and do not ask them to understand the complexities of your relationship with the other parent. That is hard enough for you, the attorneys, therapists, and parent counselors.

Be a parent, not a peer. It is easy to begin to rely on your child as a confidant and friend. Alienating parents work to get the children to line up on their side along with other friends and family. This is overwhelming for children; hence they begin to parrot their parent's viewpoints. Children have only two parents. They need you both to be in these roles. They can find plenty of peers.

Do not ask your children to divorce. This is your divorce, like it or not! The children did not ask for it, nor perhaps did they expect it. They still have the chance to maintain a relationship with both of you. They may now even have a healthier relationship with each of you than they had before.

Subtle factors can grow into big concerns. Small messages that convey to children that the other parent is not adequate or equal, does not really have any authority, is not to be trusted, or has caused pain and damage will all create an unhealthy parenting alliance. Children learn to collude with you and soon the PAS cells become cancerous. These may all be real issues, some of which need to be addressed by you as co-parents, but they don't warrant a major rift in the parent-child relationship.

Don't be so picky. You are not the perfect parent; there will be differences between the way you and your co-parent run your homes. Most of those differences are not significant. Others need to be addressed and discussed. Just remember, you cannot parent over the threshold of the other parent's home. Learn to live with the distinctions and do not make the children feel that they are doing anything bad by abiding by the more rigid or more lenient rules in the other parent's home.

Seeking Help

When parents begin to fall into the trap of parent alienation, intervention by a team of professionals is often a necessity. Many times parents need to seek their own individual therapy. Through this process they can come to understand the divorce and individual personality issues that continue to impinge on their relationships with the other parent and their children. In addition, the children usually need intervention in the form of individual and/or parent-child family therapy. This therapy helps them in two ways: to separate their own feelings from those of the alienating parent and to rebuild their relationship with the alienated parent. It is a slow and arduous process and the therapist must work together with the rest of the intervention team. It is also helpful to explore available divorce support groups for adults and children in your area. These are excellent resources for listening to others who are going through this process and for getting realistic feedback. Parent counselors are another important piece of the reunification team. They serve as monitors for parents' behavior and can report back to the court if needed. They can also provide the parent education required to parents who are traveling the path of parent alienation. They can respond directly to the parents' misbehavior by giving direct and pointed feedback when necessary. They are often in charge of coordinating all those involved in the process by organizing the feedback from all team members.

Remember that the process of parent alienation is sometimes so insidious that the intervention may be quite lengthy. By the time there is some form of intervention, especially from the courts, the alienation dynamics are often so deeply ingrained that the alienating parent and child are not even aware of them. And they're not going to be willing to relinquish their positions easily or voluntarily. In their minds, there is a great deal to lose and not much to gain. Patience and perseverance are absolutely required to reverse this process and return the divorced family to a regular co-parenting pattern. So far, the success rate for interventions in parent alienation cases has not been very high. The courts today are beginning to take a much harder stance on these issues and to recognize the seriously detrimental effects PAS can have on children's relationships from the time of alienation and well into the future.

CHAPTER 12

Healthy Parents, Healthy Children

When the Battle Is Over: "You mean I'm *really* divorced?"

Imagine not being at war. Imagine no battles, no spies, no snipers, and no sneak attacks. Imagine what you could do if your resources went to addressing the needs of your children and not to defending yourself from, or attacking, your "ex." Imagine two parents who recognize that one of the most important things they will or have ever done in their lives is to give birth to and raise their child or children. Imagine the children getting the best you both have to offer. Imagine them experiencing both of you as loving and fully dedicated to their well-being. By working toward this goal, you will teach your children that although their parents' marriage ended, the two people who love them most cared enough to stop the battle and work together. What a transition you will have achieved!

Letting go of the conflict allows you and your children to get on with your lives. It allows you the opportunity to pay attention to the lives of your children. It allows you to really focus on helping them grow and thrive without endless battles over the logistics of a parenting plan. It allows you to get back to the business of parenting.

This is truly the end of the divorce battle. Although some parents may believe that they have accepted the divorce, they are not truly acting as separate spouses. They are still embroiled in the same old battles that led to their breakup. The content may have changed slightly, but the process stays the same. For many, letting go of that hostility feels like jumping into the unknown. Fighting in one form or another is so familiar that they are not sure how to function if they don't have their ex-spouse to rail against. If they gave it up, they'd have to look at their own lives and determine their own future. Of course without that freedom they really cannot ascertain what they should do with their lives: how they want to live, who they want to be, and with whom they want to spend their time. The children have provided this last connection, the link to their old divorce world. The new co-parenting relationship is a business connection designed to raise the children into adulthood and beyond. The goal is to move forward and not to stay planted in your divorce. As one divorced parent commented, "Divorce is not a disease. Why do people keep asking me how long it has been? This is a stage in my life. I must go through it and get to the other side with my children's best interests intact."

In fact, letting go of conflict postdivorce can result in some very positive changes for you and your children. Here are a few areas where you can expect to see positive results:

Time

The amount of time spent postdivorce on legal meetings, court, therapist appointments, parent counselor meetings, evaluations for custody, writing letters, recording information, fighting with the other parent, commiserating with friends and family is phenomenal. Now you have time for yourself and for your children. Enjoy it!

Money

The amount of money spent on all of the above is also enormous. Your income will increase substantially after all the maintenance costs of a high-conflict divorce subside.

Privacy

During a high-conflict divorce, everyone knows your business. There are usually a number of people intimately involved in the process. When the divorce ends and the co-parenting battles are extinguished, all your "consultants" can be dismissed. Your life is your own again and you can maintain your own private boundaries. This is the way for you to go on with your own life.

Stress Reduction

A high-conflict divorce and subsequent co-parenting conflict take their toll on you emotionally. Symptoms of anxiety and depression are common and should decrease significantly when cooperative co-parenting is in place.

More Control

The end of the battle will allow parents more control over decision making in their own lives and those of the children. Now the court or appointed attorneys no longer have the control over when you go on vacation, whether the children play soccer, when you pick up or return the children, where and how the holidays or vacations are spent, etc. You can return to making these parental decisions yourselves.

Special Decisions Down the Road

Unfortunately, life throws us challenges. There are many decisions that parents have to make that are unanticipated, important, and difficult. There are likely to be times when you and your co-parent are faced with these decisions and do not see eye to eye. When you come upon these potential land mines in the midst of your co-parenting journey, you need to get back to basics. It's essential to really concentrate on avoiding unnecessary conflict so you can attend to your children's needs.

Perhaps more importantly, realize that you've been preparing for these decisions through your day-to-day actions with your co-parent. By building on your co-parenting conflict resolution skills, you develop a history together of solving problems. You start a pattern of creative solutions rather than a pattern of arguing and positioning for control.

Two parents with a child entering preschool and a long history of fighting over details large and small began to discuss why the mother had signed the child up for school only on days when the child had not been with the father the night before. This clearly could be an attempt for the mother to deprive the child and the father of the opportunity for Dad's involvement in preschool. Dad could not leave work in the middle of the day to pick the child up, so therefore he could not be involved unless he could take the child to school in the morning. He requested that Mom change the days so that he could take the child to school on "his" days. This could have easily become a major struggle for these parents, until Mom offered a solution. "How about you taking [child] to school one day a week? That way you can meet his teacher, stay for a while, and get involved. If it is the same day each week, we can plan for it and it can be part of the routine." A perfect solution was crafted in a minute or two, without conflict! These parents stepped around the land mine that this special situation created.

They avoided the conflict by concentrating on the ultimate goals and logistics that would achieve the desired result, rather than focusing on the assumed motives of the other parent. The father could have assumed the mother was trying to keep him away from this important part of the child's life. The mother could have assumed that the father was trying to control every decision and use this as an opportunity to further infringe on "her" days with the child. Instead, they focused on simply addressing the matter at hand: "How do we give [child] a chance to have Dad involved in preschool?" By keeping the problem focused in this way they solved it effectively, quickly, and without conflict.

Finding a Parent Counselor and Other Resources

Parents in intact families use friends, therapists, family, teachers, physicians, clergy, and other resources to help with parenting decisions. Unfortunately, it's not often that divorced parents consult a resource together as co-parents. And when they talk to the same resource at separate times, they often get two different impressions. "That's not at all what Dr. Jones told me," they will say to one another. "I heard just the opposite of what you did." Furthermore, when they seek input from their own particular support network of family and friends, they often experience the support in a way that can easily reestablish the conflict, as these individuals take sides. Support networks tend to take sides early on, especially during the worst of the conflict. They are probably still viewing you in the conflict and are still trying to help you fight the battles.

Input should be sought from individuals who can offer advice based on the needs of the children rather than from the standpoint of who is the better parent or the "good guy" or "bad guy." Whether you rely on professional or personal sources, you as parents need to assess how committed and able these individuals are at really focusing on the needs of the children.

One set of professionals who can be helpful is parent counselors. Often these people are psychologists and therapists. But they don't help you by offering therapy. Rather, they apply their knowledge of parenting strategies, child development, communication, and problem solving to the matters at hand. They should be able to give you input on a specific decision, rather than telling you who is right or wrong, or trying to help you discover all the psychodynamic reasons for your taking a certain position as a parent. Parent counselors do not, in this role, provide treatment of a mental disorder. They provide consultation to help parents make reasonable decisions with regard to their children. They may not even see your children, as they believe that ultimately you know your children the best. The parent counselor's role is to consult with you to make sure your thinking seems reasonable and that you haven't failed to consider important elements with regard to the decisions you are trying to make. Once you have resolved the conflict and learned the appropriate skills for listening and decision making, you might still seek a parent counselor's opinion again from time to time around special decisions. At that time it may only require one, two, or three meetings to move beyond a certain situation. It is not therapy, and you don't have to invest the same level of emotional commitment, time, and money.

Whether you use a parent counselor or another resource, the key is to see to it that this person does not cause more conflict. They need to take the side of your child (not one or another of the parents). They need to be focused on solving the problem at hand and helping you look at the reasonableness of the options in front of you. They need to leave the parenting decisions to you and your co-parent and not attempt to make the decision for you. In short, they need to allow you and your co-parent to truly parent your children together.

There are also some excellent group programs for parents administered by individual state agencies and privately. The efficacy, length of intervention, choice of treatment format, and size of group depend upon the level of conflict (Blaisure and Geasler 2000).

There Is Hope

Breaking the addiction to conflict is simply about behavior and choice. It is unlike many other addictions in that there is no chemical or physical dependency. Nicotine, alcohol, caffeine, heroin, and most other addictions have such a strong hold on a person because of the combination of psychological dependency and the physical addiction. The recovery from conflict addiction is not about what you feel. It is, as we stated earlier in this book, about what you do. Building a collaborative co-parenting relationship is simply about parents insisting that they themselves act and communicate with each other and their children in a civil and responsible manner. You are in control of this, and there is hope. Your children are the beneficiaries or the victims of your behavior, and the stakes are too high for you to make the wrong choice. Choose civility and your children have a better chance to thrive. Choose conflict and your children lose out in many ways. It *is* in your hands. If you are focused on your own choices (not the choices of your co-parent), then you *can* make better decisions that will avert a great deal of the potential conflict. You may not be perfect (nor may your co-parent) but you *can* do your best.

Congratulations! Your Children Have Their Parents Back

As you could see throughout this book, when parents are stuck in conflict, they become preoccupied with the battles they face. They look for the flaws in each other and they position themselves to avoid what they perceive as "losing" the many battles that arise. They concentrate on their co-parent's actions and are so focused on them that they might as well still be living together. When you kick the conflict addiction habit, you return home to your children. You are not distracted by your own anger and hurt and by your co-parent's behavior. Instead your children finally return to having two parents who can talk, plan, and solve their problems.

Your children may be children of divorce, but they do not have to be victims of divorce. They deserve to feel loved and cherished.

Resources

Divorce Parenting Web Sites

These are some suggestions—or just search on "Co-Parenting Divorce"

www.spig.clara.net
Shared Parenting Information Group (SPIG) UK, promoting responsi-ble shared parenting after separation and divorce.

www.divorceinfo.net/coparent.html
Decrease the stress of your divorce. Sample of co-parenting agree-ment.

www.divorcesource.com
Comprehensive divorce information and advice relating to custody, visitation, child support and other issues related to children and divorce.

www.cyfc.umn.edu
Coparenting Ten Commandments, May 1995.

www.ncoff.gse.upenn.edu
The CoParenting Library.

www.betterdivorce.com
Parenting and other information on divorce.

www.hec.ohio-state.edu
Parenting issues in divorcing families.

www.flying-solo.com
Divorce information for individuals and parents.

www.kidshare.com
Co-parenting information.

www.divorce-online.com
Electronic journal on a variety of divorce issues.

www.kidsinthemiddle.com
Information on the effects of divorce on children.

Suggested Readings

American Bar Association. 1998. Coparenting after divorce. *Family Advocate* 21:11-56.

Baris, M., and C. Garrity. 1988. *Children of Divorce*. Asheville, N.C.: Psytec Corp.

Blau, M. 1993. *Families Apart*. New York: Berkley Publishing Group.

Blau, M. 1996. *Loving and Listening*. New York: Berkley Publishing Group.

Darnall, D. 1998. *Divorce Casualties*. Dallas: Taylor Publishing Company.

Ehrenberg, M. 1996. Cooperative parenting arrangements after marital separation: former couples who make it work. *Journal of Divorce and Remarriage* 26:93-115.

Ehrenberg, M., and M. Elterman. 1966. Shared parenting agreements after marital separation: The roles of empathy and narcissism. *Journal of Consulting and Clinical Psychology* 64:808-818.

Gardner, R. 1998. *The Parental Alienation Syndrome: A Guide for Mental Health and Legal Professionals, (2nd ed.).* Cresskill, N. J.: Creative Therapeutics, Inc.

Garrity, C., and M. Baris. 1994. *Caught in the Middle.* San Francisco: Jossey-Bass Publishers.

Goldstein, J., A. Solnit, S. Goldstein, and A. Freud. 1996. *The Best Interests of the Child.* New York: The Free Press.

Krementz, J. 1996. *How It Feels When Parents Divorce.* New York: Alfred A. Knopf.

Lansky, V. 1996. *Divorce Book for Parents.* Deephaven, Minn.: The Book Peddlers.

Lewis, J., and W. Sammon. 1999. *Don't Divorce Your Children.* Lincolnwood, Ill.: Contemporary Books.

McBride, B., and T. Rane. 1998. Parenting alliance as a predictor of father involvement: an exploratory study. *Family Relations* 47:229-236.

McKay, M., P. Rogers, J. Blades, and R. Gosse. 1999. *The Divorce Book.* Oakland, Calif.: New Harbinger Publications.

Pam, A., and J. Pearson. 1998. *Splitting Up.* New York: The Guilford Press.

Pruett, M., and K. Hoganbruen. 1998. Joint custody and shared parenting, research and interventions. *Child and Adolescent Psychiatric Clinics of North America* 7:273-294.

Ricci, I. 1997. *Mom's House, Dad's House.* New York: Simon and Schuster.

Schneider, M., and J. Zuckerberg. 1996. *Difficult Questions Kids Ask (and Are Too Afraid to Ask) About Divorce.* New York: Simon & Schuster Inc.

Stewart, A., A. Copeland, N. Chester, J. Malley, and N. Barenbaum. 1997. *Separating Together. How Divorce Transforms Families.* New York: The Guilford Press.

Teyber, E. 1992. *Helping Children Cope with Divorce.* San Francisco: Jossey-Bass Publishers.

Wallerstein, J., and S. Blakeslee. 1996. *Second Chances.* Boston: Houghton Miffin Co.

Wallerstein, J., and J. Kelly. 1996. *Surviving the Breakup.* New York: Basic Books.

References

Barstow, D. 2000. Behind a murder suspect's cool facade, emotional turmoil. *New York Times*, February 5, B1.

Blaisure, K., and M. Geasler. 2000. The Divorce Education Intervention Model. *Family and Conciliation Courts Review* 38:501-513.

Blau, M. 1993. *Families Apart: Ten Keys to Successful Co-Parenting.* New York: The Berkley Publishing Group.

Blau, M. 1996. *Loving and Listening.* New York: The Berkley Publishing Group.

Darnall, D. 1998. *Divorce Casualties: Protecting Your Children From Parental Alienation.* Dallas: Taylor Publishing Company.

Ellis, E. 2000. *Divorce Wars: Interventions with Families in Conflict.* Washington, D.C.: American Psychological Association.

Gardner, R. 1998. *The Parental Alienation Syndrome: A Guide for Mental Health and Legal Professionals, (2nd ed.).* Cresskill, N.J.: Creative Therapeutics, Inc.

Garrity, C., and M. Baris. 1994. *Caught in the Middle: Protecting the Children of High-Conflict Divorce.* San Francisco: Jossey-Bass Publishers.

Ricci, I. 1980. *Mom's House, Dad's House: Making Shared Custody Work.* New York: Macmillan.

Wallerstein, J., J. Lewis, and S. Blakeslee. 2000. *The Unexpected Legacy of Divorce.* New York: Hyperion.

Wallerstein, J., and J. Kelly. 1980. *Surviving the Breakup: How Parents and Children Cope with Divorce.* New York: Basic Books.

Elizabeth Thayer, Ph.D., is Vice-President and Cofounder of Beacon Behavioral Services, LLC (Avon, CT) and the P.E.A.C.E. Program (Parents Equally Allied to Co-parent Effectively), which is a specialized service for high-conflict divorced and divorcing parents. She is a member of the American Psychological Association and Connecticut Psychological Association. She serves on the State of Connecticut Board of Examiners in Psychology and as Chair of the Certification of Professional Qualifications Appeals Committee of the Association of State and Provincial Psychology Boards.

Jeffrey Zimmerman, Ph.D., is President and Cofounder of Beacon Behavioral Services, LLC (Avon, CT) and the P.E.A.C.E. Program (Parents Equally Allied to Co-parent Effectively), which is a specialized service for high-conflict divorced and divorcing parents. He is a member of the American Psychological Association and a member, Past President, and Fellow of the Connecticut Psychological Association.

He is also a Diplomate and Founding Fellow of the American College of Advanced Practice Psychologists and is on the clinical faculty of the University of Connecticut Health Center.

For more information on the P.E.A.C.E. program or on training opportunities for professionals contact Drs. Thayer and Zimmerman at:

Beacon Behavioral Services, LLC
40 Dale Road, suite 201
Avon, CT 06001
860-676-9350
jzimmerman@beaconbehavioral.com

Some Other
New Harbinger Titles

Helping A Child with Nonverbal Learning Disorder, 2nd edition
Item 5266 $15.95

The Introvert & Extrovert in Love, Item 4863 $14.95

Helping Your Socially Vulnerable Child, Item 4580 $15.95

Life Planning for Adults with Developmental Disabilities, Item 4511 $19.95

But I Didn't Mean That! Item 4887 $14.95

The Family Intervention Guide to Mental Illness, Item 5068 $17.95

It's So Hard to Love You, Item 4962 $14.95

The Turbulent Twenties, Item 4216 $14.95

The Balanced Mom, Item 4534 $14.95

Helping Your Child Overcome Separation Anxiety & School Refusal,
Item 4313 $14.95

When Your Child Is Cutting, Item 4375 $15.95

Helping Your Child with Selective Mutism, Item 416X $14.95

Sun Protection for Life, Item 4194 $11.95

Helping Your Child with Autism Spectrum Disorder, Item 3848 $17.95

Teach Me to Say It Right, Item 4038 $13.95

Grieving Mindfully, Item 4011 $14.95

The Courage to Trust, Item 3805 $14.95

The Gift of ADHD, Item 3899 $14.95

The Power of Two Workbook, Item 3341 $19.95

Adult Children of Divorce, Item 3368 $14.95

*Fifty Great Tips, Tricks, and Techniques to Connect
with Your Teen,* Item 3597 $10.95

Helping Your Child with OCD, Item 3325 $19.95

Helping Your Depressed Child, Item 3228 $14.95

Call **toll free, 1-800-748-6273,** or log on to our online bookstore at
www.newharbinger.com to order. Have your Visa or Mastercard number ready. Or send a check for the titles you want to New Harbinger
Publications, Inc., 5674 Shattuck Ave., Oakland, CA 94609. Include $4.50
for the first book and 75¢ for each additional book, to cover shipping
and handling. (California residents please include appropriate sales tax.)
Allow two to five weeks for delivery.

Prices subject to change without notice.